THE CADEN CHRONICLES

# DEAD LOW TIDE

## Also by Eddie Jones

### The Caden Chronicles

*Dead Man's Hand (Book 1)*

*Skull Creek Stakeout (Book 2)*

*The Curse of Captain LaFoote*

*My Father's Business: 30 Inspirational Stories
for Discerning and Doing God's Will*

THE CADEN CHRONICLES

# DEAD LOW TIDE

BOOK THREE

## EDDIE JONES

ZONDERkidz

We want to hear from you. Please send your comments about this book to us in care of zreview@zondervan.com. Thank you.

ZONDERKIDZ

*Dead Low Tide*

Copyright © 2013 by Eddie Jones

This title is also available as a Zondervan ebook.

Visit www.zondervan.com/ebooks

Requests for information should be addressed to:

Zonderkidz, 5300 Patterson Ave SE, Grand Rapids, Michigan 49530

Library of Congress Cataloging-in-Publication Data

Jones, Eddie, 1957–
    Dead low tide / Eddie Jones.
      pages cm. – (The Caden chronicles ; book three)
    Summary: "On vacation with his parents in Savannah, Georgia, Nick Caden is eager to investigate the mystery surrounding Heidi May Laveau, a girl who supposedly died years ago but whose body just washed up on the shore" – Provided by publisher.
    ISBN 978-0-310-72392-9 (softcover)
    [1. Supernatural–Fiction. 2. Zombies–Fiction. 3. Kidnapping–Fiction. 4. Brothers and sisters–Fiction. 5. Savannah (Ga.)–Fiction. 6. Mystery and detective stories.] I. Title.
PZ7.J68534Dds 2014
[Fic]–dc23                                        2013034792

Published in association with Hartline Literary Agency, 123 Queenston Drive, Pittsburgh, PA 15235. www.hartlineliterary.com.

Zonderkidz is a trademark of Zondervan.

*Cover design: Sammy Yuen*
*Editor: Kim Childress*
*Illustrations: Owen Richardson*
*Interior design: Sarah Molegraaf*
*Interior composition: Greg Johnson/Textbook Perfect*

Printed in the United States of America

13 14 15 16 17 18 19 /DCI/ 20 19 18 17 16 15 14 13 12 11 10 9 8 7 6 5 4 3 2 1

*I dedicate* Dead Low Tide *to my editor, Kim Childress, for putting up with me and giving me a chance.*
*Thanks Kim.*

# CONTENTS

# CHAPTER ONE
# DANGER AT DEAD LOW TIDE

**October 31**
**Palmetto Island, Savannah, Georgia**
**8:27 p.m.**

Three days ago, a local fisherman discovered the body of Heidi May Laveau lying facedown on a muddy oyster bed in Savage Creek. The fisherman, whose name has not been released, told authorities he was setting a crab trap when he noticed what appeared to be a bottle-nose porpoise washed up onshore.

"But when I got close I knowed it warn't no dead dolphin. Stank so bad it liked to gagged me."

The fisherman described the victim as wearing a sleeveless white dress, a soggy wrist corsage, and a "bad

case of crabs, if you get my drift. One look at the crabs
crawling all over her face and I liked to have lost my
grits," the fisherman is reported to have said.

I paused and examined the previous sentence ... *The fisherman is reported to have said* ... With a couple of keystrokes
I deleted the passive phrase and automatically saved the story
onto our cloud server.

I'm an okay writer but not great, and that's a bad thing
when you're a reporter for one of the web's hottest alternate
reality news outlets. The Laveau case marked my nine-month
anniversary of writing for the *Cool Ghoul Gazette*, an online
magazine covering strange paranormal events and occult-like
activities. I try to keep the bloody descriptions to a minimum,
but I still get complaints (from moms, mostly) that my writing
is too graphic and gory. So let me just say this right here, right
now: If you're the sort of reader who gets queasy at the mention
of bodies oozing blood or corpses with eyes gouged out and
bones poking through skin, then STOP READING RIGHT
NOW! The Laveau case involves voodoo, curses, black magic,
disembodied spirits, the walking dead, and a seriously disturb-
ing scene involving a goat.

There, don't say I didn't warn you.

From the abandoned boathouse on Savage Creek, I studied
the blackened mud flat where the body was rumored to have
appeared. I say rumored because, other than the eyewitness, no
one has seen the corpse. Mist blanketed Savage Island, making
it impossible to see anything more than the shoreline and the

tops of the palmetto trees. On the sand not thirty yards away lay our bikes with handlebars and fenders glimmering beneath a crescent moon. Slanting dock pilings sprouted from the sand and extended into black water—the remainder of the pier having been washed away by a recent storm.

That's why I'd "borrowed" the canoe. We needed a way to get out to the weathered boathouse.

"Mom and Dad are gonna freak when they come back and find us gone."

I glanced at Wendy. My sister sat on the floor of the boathouse not three feet from me. Every time she opened her mouth she sounded like a frog being strangled.

Normally I work alone when investigating a homicide. And that's what this was—a cold case with a colder corpse. But that night I brought her along on the stakeout. So there we were, hiding in the boathouse, waiting for the tide—and my life—to turn.

"We'll go in a few minutes," I answered.

"Come on, Nick. You're not going to see a dead body, not tonight, anyway. The only thing dying out here is me ... from boredom."

"Good one, sis." Wendy had picked up a nasty cold before we left Kansas and it had turned into laryngitis. Still, her croaking attempt at humor made me smile. "Five more minutes, then we'll go."

"You said that five minutes ago."

"It's not like I can control the moon's gravitational pull, you know."

"This isn't going to be like that vampire story you wrote, is it, where you almost got killed?"

"Article," I said, correcting Wendy. "Stories aren't necessarily based on facts."

"And a zombie sighting is?"

Ignoring my sister's sarcasm, I went back to work on my article.

Laveau was a member of the National Honor Society, president of her church youth group, and served as captain of her varsity cheerleading squad. The evening of her death—nearly fifteen years ago—she attended an award ceremony aboard the *Southern Belle*, a riverboat that sails from the downtown Savannah waterfront. As the vessel passed Savage Island, Laveau strolled toward the back of the boat.

Accounts from numerous eyewitnesses confirm the young woman climbed over a side railing and, with a wave to onlookers, jumped into the Savannah River. She surfaced in the paddle wheel's wake and began swimming toward shore, but the driver of a Jet Ski accidentally ran her over. Laveau's family buried the young woman in Savannah's Bonaventure Memorial Gardens, a cemetery nicknamed "The City of the Dead."

"Thing that's got me puzzled," said the unnamed fisherman, "is after I seen the body I ran my boat back to the marina to get help, but when I come back with the marine patrol there warn't nothing on that oyster bed no more. I could see a body washing away if the tide was coming in, maybe. But going out? Don't make no sense."

The fisherman's eyewitness account leaves this reporter wondering how, exactly, a dead person from fifteen years ago ended up on an oyster bed at dead low tide. And if she was on that oyster bed, where is she now?

"I don't think Dad's going to get the job."

Wendy's comment interrupted my typing. I hit Save and looked up. "Palmetto Island Realty wouldn't have put us up for two nights in the condo if they weren't serious about hiring Dad."

"But what does Dad know about selling real estate? I bet the only reason that real estate lady took Mom and Dad to dinner was to try and sell them one of those condos."

That thought had occurred to me, too. As a plant production consultant, Dad is good at helping manufacturing plants run more efficiently, but selling resort property to retiring Baby Boomers? I just couldn't see it. Thing is, Dad needs work. He lost his job early last summer as a plant consultant. Lost it right after we got home from Transylvania, North Carolina, where I solved the vampire murder. Thank goodness we sold our house in Lawrence, Kansas, right away, because my parents could never make the mortgage payment on Mom's salary alone.

Actually, Mom was the one who sold our house. She has her real estate license; Dad's just got big ideas. Mom got a good offer before she even listed it. The day of the closing we put all our furniture and stuff in storage and went to live in Aunt Molly and Uncle Eric's cabin on Milford Lake, just north of Junction City. The cabin is pretty nice. No heat or A/C. Just lots of windows looking out onto the lake. But it's definitely not some place you want to be during a Kansas winter. That's why we have to move out—and Dad was so anxious to interview for the real estate job on Palmetto Island. I felt better knowing Mom was with Dad at the dinner meeting. Dad is the eternal optimist in the family, Mom the level-headed one. My father is always talking about how our ship is about to come in, whereas Mom is convinced the Cadens' ship sank years ago.

Scratching a bug bite on her arm, my sister said, "The other night I heard Mom on the phone with Aunt Molly. The two of them were talking about how Mom and me might spend the winter with Uncle Eric and Aunt Molly. Just until Dad can find work, Mom said. If that happens, I bet I end up sleeping on the floor in one of the twins' bedrooms."

"I thought you liked hanging out with your cousins."

"Yeah, right. Who wouldn't like sharing a room with Diva Eva and Drama Donna?"

I smiled, thinking of how Wendy was like Mom and quick to see past people's phoniness.

I didn't dare tell Wendy what I really thought: that Mom was considering leaving Dad for good. Things between Mom and Dad have been going downhill for a long time. Almost since Wendy could walk. The first couple of times they yelled at each other, I went running into my room and hid under my bed. But then it started happening so often I got used to it. On the drive to Palmetto Island my parents had kept their carping to a minimum, but we all knew Dad's interview with Palmetto Island Realty was a huge deal. Not just for the two of them but all of us. I was pretty sure my parents still loved each other. But

Mom lets things get the best of her and takes it out on Dad. Things like paying the bills and not having enough money to buy groceries.

"If you have to sleep with one of the twins, it'll only be for a little while," I said, trying to sound hopeful.

"I'd rather live in our car."

"You say that now, but wait until you have to curl up in the trunk to get away from Dad's snoring." I reached into my pocket and tossed Wendy a throat lozenge. "It'll all work out, sis, you'll see."

Farther up the beach, a group of teens sat around a bonfire. From the way they were talking—loud and falling all over each other—it appeared they'd been drinking. *Dumb idea,* I thought. *Especially near where Laveau's body washed up … and vanished. And on the eve of Savannah's annual zombie festival, too.*

Wendy popped the lozenge in her mouth and scooted toward the trapdoor. "I'm going to wait in the canoe."

"Don't, I need you to stay here."

Ignoring me, Wendy lifted the canvas flap that covered the hole in the floor of the boathouse and backed down the ladder. She was all the way to the floating dock before I leaned over the top of the ladder and held out the canoe paddle. "You're going to need one of these."

"Toss it down."

"Nope. Not until I say we're ready to go." With my sister frowning at me, I went back to writing my article.

According to eyewitnesses, there were no footprints around the place where Laveau's body supposedly appeared, making the gruesome discovery even more bizarre. This is not the first case of a corpse mysteriously washing up on a muddy creek bank. After Hurricane Katrina, corpses floated from shallow graves and were found scattered throughout New Orleans. But this reporter thinks there is more to this case than heavy rains and cemeteries built at sea level.

"Ah, Nick?"

Nor does the Laveau sighting mean the town of Savannah is about to be invaded by real flesh-eating zombies — as some other news outlets have suggested.

"I'm not kidding, get down here!"

But the fact remains that the "remains" of something or someone washed up on Savage Creek, so readers are encouraged to check back tomorrow for the second installment in the mysterious Heidi May Laveau case.

"NICK!"

I hit Control S and looked down at the dock. The aluminum canoe no longer floated next to the dock. I lay flat on my belly and leaned over the edge of the trapdoor. Wendy knelt in the middle of the canoe, both hands flailing at the water while she frantically tried to paddle back to the dock.

"Cuss a monkey." I backed down the ladder. "I told you to wait," I said under my breath.

As soon as my feet hit the dock, I leaned out and tried to grab the canoe, but it was already too far away. "Why did you untie the dock line?"

"I didn't!"

"Oh right. I guess the canoe just untied itself."

Wendy kept trying to hand-paddle back to the dock but the current was too strong. Before she drifted completely out of range, I hurried up the ladder and grabbed the boat oar and came back down. Using the narrow handle end, I tried to hook the front of the canoe but missed.

"Just toss it to me!" Wendy demanded.

"And if I miss?"

"Would you just throw it?"

The oar banged off the side and floated away — just as I'd feared.

For a second or two I thought about jumping in. The canoe was only a few feet away from the dock. But then I'd have to swim back to the beach and ride home soaking wet. Besides which, my tablet and backpack and cell phone were still in the boathouse and I had no idea how I would get them to shore.

I was still trying to come up with another way to lasso the canoe when bubbles floated up next to the dock. It was only a few at first. Then a whole line of them moving toward the canoe. *Oh, great! An alligator*, I thought. We'd been warned by a woman at the rental office to stay clear of the pond out back of our condo. "A lot of times you'll see gators sunning on the bank during the day, but don't go near them. They may look slow and lazy, but they can run up to thirty-five miles an hour."

But it wasn't a gator.

Looking back on things now, I wish it had been.

The moon sailed from behind clouds, and as it did, Heidi May Laveau bubbled up from the depths of the black creek.

The body floated facedown, arms out, with rotting skin flaking off like chunks of confetti. Her white dress showed pale white in the moon's glow. Dark hair covered the portion of her scalp not caved in by the Jet Ski all those years ago. A gash across her shoulder exposed the jagged end of a broken bone.

Thank goodness Wendy had her back to me. Otherwise she'd have freaked. Instead, she'd bent over the side of the canoe and was still trying to get the canoe turned around and headed toward the beach.

*Think, Nick, think.* My mind raced a thousand miles a minute as I considered my options. I finally came up with ... panic.

The current carried the corpse into the canoe. Laveau's shoulder bumped against the silver hull.

"Wendy, don't move," I whispered.

"What?"

"Stop splashing." I was too afraid to speak louder.

"But I have to—" She whirled and saw the body floating next to the canoe.

With a startling quickness the corpse came alive.

A grisly hand shot from the water and clamped bony fingers

onto the canoe. Wendy screamed but the laryngitis reduced her shrieking to a hissing whisper. Purple-black feet surfaced behind the dress and kicked, pushing my sister away from me — away from the dock and toward the fog.

"Wendy!" I teetered on the edge of the dock. "Jump in! I'll toss a life jacket to you!"

"Nick, do something!" she yelled in a wheezing screech.

Grizzled gray fingers reached for my sister's throat. "Wendy, jump!"

"I—"

Skeletal fingers clamped over my sister's mouth; her muffled screams fell silent. In horror I watched as the canoe, my sister, and the stinking corpse of Heidi May Laveau glided into the bank of fog. For several agonizing seconds I watched my sister struggling to break free of the dead hand clamped across her mouth.

Then she vanished into the mist.

I stood frozen to the dock, unable to breathe. A final passing thought flashed through my mind as I jumped in and began swimming to shore to get help. *Ah, man, how am I going to explain to my parents that a zombie took Wendy?*

# CHAPTER TWO
# DEAD AND GONE

What do you mean you lost your sister?"

I straddled my bike in front of our rented condo. Dad hadn't even let me get off before he grabbed me by the shoulders and started yelling at me.

"Dad, you have to believe me, it wasn't my fault. I told her to wait for me but she got in the canoe, and a dead—"

"What were you doing down at that creek is what I want to know!"

Telling Dad I'd gone hunting for another *Cool Ghoul* story would only make things worse. He was already plenty mad; I could tell that from the way he'd gone ballistic and started yelling at me when I rode up. I looked away from his hard gaze and studied the bike's chrome fender.

"Well? I'm waiting," Dad huffed.

"Dad, I'm sorry, but it happened so fast. One minute she was in the canoe floating away from the dock; the next, that thing had her." Just saying it out loud made me queasy. Before then I'd been working off adrenaline but now, standing before Dad, I felt like any second I'd hurl. "I told her not to get into the canoe but she wouldn't listen."

"Don't try to blame this on your sister. It's your fault! The two of you were supposed to stay here—that was the deal."

"Police are on the way," said Mom, butting in. "Frank, are you driving or am I?"

Dad released my shoulders and stared blankly at Mom as though he'd forgotten she was there.

"Fine, I'll drive," Mom said coolly. She marched to the driver's side of the Buick and slid behind the wheel.

I could tell she was working on autopilot, processing the situation and setting things in motion. While Dad screamed in my face, Mom had calmly demanded I tell her the exact time Wendy went missing ("I dunno, Mom, probably like a quarter to nine"), phoned the emergency operator, and checked the condo to make sure it was locked. My mother would fall apart later when she was no longer in charge.

"You two coming?"

We piled into the Buick. Mom and Dad in the front, me slumped in the back seat. With both hands on the wheel, Mom backed out of the parking space and raced out of the parking lot. She knew the way to the marina. Or, sort of knew. At Dad's insistence we'd spent part of the afternoon checking out boats. But I could tell from the way she kept slowing down to read street signs that she wasn't 100 percent sure of where the turn was.

"Nick, this has to stop." Mom glared at me in the rearview mirror.

I braced myself for Mom's lecture. Normally Dad's the calm one, but when it's something really bad, Mom becomes quiet, stews, and then unloads with both barrels.

"No more ghosts. No more vampires and zombies, do you hear me? You're done writing for that website."

I leaned forward and pointed at the windshield. "Turn at that sign."

"Did you hear your mother?"

"Yeah, Dad, I heard."

"Don't take that tone," said Mom. "You're in plenty enough trouble as it is."

I almost started to explain (again) that Wendy's disappearance wasn't *all* my fault. That she and the zombie-thing shared some blame, but instead I kept my mouth shut. Not that my parents cared, but I felt horrible. It had been my idea to go to the boathouse. My editor, Calvin, had suggested the Laveau incident might make for an interesting article. He hadn't exactly promised front-page placement on the website, but I knew with the right pictures it was a possibility. That's why I'd wanted to go at low tide. To snap some pics and video with my tablet.

Mom swung the Buick into the marina parking lot and jumped out. A fleet of expensive-looking motor yachts and sailboats greeted us on the main dock. Floodlights illuminated a walkway as the three of us hurried past the marina basin and down to the creek. One look at the crime-scene tape blocking access to the pier's busted dock pilings and Mom lost it.

"This is your fault! You're the reason he's like this!"

"Me?" said Dad, rounding on Mom.

"Yes, you, Frank. If you weren't so busy trying to be Nick's buddy instead of his father . . ."

I felt about an inch tall. Dad and I *had* become closer over the past year. Our buddy-buddy time began after our trip out west to Deadwood Canyon. Before then, the two of us could hardly stand to be in the same room. But after I'd solved the mystery surrounding the identity of Billy the Kid's killer, Dad began treating me differently. "Not every fifteen-year-old gets a write-up in *Police Blotter* magazine," he'd bragged to me. "You keep on solving cases and one day maybe you'll be able to make a living doing this."

Now Dad only looked disappointed.

Mom jogged up the beach to where the uniformed officer stood questioning a group of teens.

"You have to find my daughter," I heard her say to the officer as we walked up. "You just have to."

Mom had inserted herself between the officer and a girl who appeared to be about my age. The teen wore a baggy denim shirt, jeans, and bright red flip-flops.

"I'm afraid there isn't much we can do right now, ma'am. We're just getting started on the search."

The young woman quickly glanced my direction, then wandered back to join her friends by the campfire.

The officer introduced himself as Officer McDonald and pointed toward a marine patrol boat motoring past the boathouse. A uniformed officer leaned over the side of the boat as though searching the water for a body. "We hope to know more in a few minutes."

"Oh my gosh, don't tell me you think she drowned. Is that what you're saying? That my daughter has drowned?"

Dad sidled over and placed a hand on Mom's shoulder. "Sylvia, please. That's not what he said."

Quickly Mom slapped Dad's hand away.

Dad said to the officer, "I'm afraid we don't know much other than what my son told us. He claims our daughter was in a canoe that drifted away from that dock."

"Didn't drift," I corrected him. "Was pushed."

The officer jerked his chin in the direction of the teens. "The girl I was speaking with said she heard talking in the boathouse. Walked down the beach to check, heard a splash, and saw someone riding away on a bike."

"That was me."

Officer McDonald eyed me skeptically. "You were there, you saw what happened?"

"Yes, sir."

"He was with my daughter," Mom cut in.

*My* daughter. As though she already had custody of Wendy. As though my parents were already divorced.

"If you don't mind, I'd like to speak to your son."

"Sure. Nick, tell the officer what happened," Dad said.

"Alone, if you don't mind."

Before my parents could object, Officer McDonald walked me toward a makeshift command center, complete with tent, floodlights, and generator. Electrical cords snaked across sand. News crews began arriving. Already the dune separating the narrow beach from the golf course fairway was clogged with curious onlookers.

"Don't suppose you know anything about a canoe that went missing from the outdoor rec center?" Officer McDonald's pale-green eyes looked at me from beneath the brim of a tan patrol hat. He had a broad-shouldered, muscular build that strained the buttons on his crisp brown uniform.

"We only needed to borrow it long enough to paddle out to the boathouse," I explained. "I was going to put it back as soon as we were done."

"How, is what I want to know? Those canoes are chained to the rack."

"Picked the lock."

He eyed me skeptically. "You?"

"In my backpack is a KLOM lock pick set. Best forty bucks I ever spent. Takes some practice to learn how to trip the tumblers, but I've gotten pretty good at it."

"You say that like it's something to be proud of."

"No, not really, it's just that ... I needed to get out to that boathouse."

"Oh, why's that?"

I completely skipped over the part about wanting to see the spot where Heidi May Laveau had washed up days before and instead recounted how Wendy and I were killing time while our parents were at dinner. I told the officer my sister got bored, stepped into the canoe, and it floated off. When I got to the part about the body floating up, Officer McDonald stopped me.

"Run that last part by me again?"

"The person who took my sister was dressed like a zombie."

"Sure it wasn't a stump or a log floating?"

"It had hands and feet and a head. And it was wearing a dress. Look, I know it wasn't a real zombie, okay? There's no such thing. But it *is* my fault my sister is missing. I'm the one who talked her into coming with me to the boathouse. Come on, let me help. I can find her, I know I can. Put me in one of those patrol boats."

"No chance of that happening," Officer McDonald replied coolly. "I'm still trying to decide if I should charge you with theft."

"But I'm the only one who saw which way they went. Please? Wendy's probably scared out of her gourd right now."

Officer McDonald walked behind the generator and returned with my backpack, handing it to me. "You might want to consider getting rid of that lock picking set."

"Yes, sir. Good idea."

"Why is everyone still standing around?" Mom demanded, waving her arms at the officers standing around under the tent. "Shouldn't they be looking for my little girl?"

"There's a bird in the air. Should be along any minute," answered Officer McDonald. "If that canoe is in the creek, we'll find her with that big spotlight. You can count on it."

"By bird, you mean a helicopter?" said Mom anxiously. "Where is it? I don't hear anything. Wouldn't I hear it if it was on the way?"

Officer McDonald pointed toward a bright light approaching from the west. "Look, I know you're worried. If it were my daughter, I would be, too. But the local radio station is always coming up with crazy stunts to boost their ratings. Starting tomorrow there's a zombie festival in Savannah. Could be that some DJ got a little too carried away."

"Are you saying this is somebody's idea of a joke?"

"I'm not saying one way or the other. I won't know for sure what we're dealing with until we get more boats in the water. In the meantime, I've called in a canine unit. It would be helpful if you would let their dogs go through some of your daughter's things. You know, in case she's stuck on that island and hiking around trying to find a way off."

"Frank, take Nick back to the condo and get him out of those smelly clothes. You two can wait for this dog squad. I'll stay here."

"I wish I could let you do that, ma'am, but we need everyone off this beach except official personnel. I'll have one of my officers follow you back to where you're staying."

"But I want—"

"Come on, Sylvia, let the man do his job."

Mom jerked her hand from Dad's. "Fine. But I'm not waiting around in that condo all night. If I don't hear something about my daughter soon, I'm coming back, and when I do, it'll take a lot more than a couple of officers to keep me away."

Mom and Dad started up the beach toward the marina parking lot. I fell in behind, then felt Officer McDonald tapping me on the shoulder. I paused and turned.

"That fellow standing over by the cart path?"

I looked to see where Officer McDonald was pointing. All I could make out was the silhouette of a person.

"He runs the Outdoor Activities Recreational Center. Came on board last summer after we had some trouble with vandalism and petty theft. Windsurfers and kiteboards and such kept walking off. If I was you, I'd apologize to him for taking that canoe."

"Yes, sir. I will."

"But you might want to wait until we get it back, first."

*You mean if you get it back.*

## CHAPTER THREE
# AN INVITATION TO TROUBLE

**H**ow'd the dinner go?"

The Buick remained deadly quiet on the ride back to the condo. No matter how many times I apologized for dragging Wendy down to the boathouse (I was working on my third apology), Mom and Dad couldn't seem to bring themselves to forgive me. I couldn't blame them, really. Saying you're sorry and meaning it aren't the same, and lately I'd made it a habit of doing things against my parents' wishes.

Dad answered my question about dinner by asking (*again*) what I was doing in an abandoned boathouse with my sister when we'd both been ordered not to leave the condo.

"Told you, I was working on an article for *Cool Ghoul Gazette*." Trying to change the subject, I asked, "Did they make you an offer?"

Dad, wearing a serious scowl on his face, studied me in the rearview mirror. Mom sat in the passenger seat, her head resting against the window. I couldn't tell if she was crying, but the way she kept putting her hand to her face led me to believe she was.

"Come on, Dad, give me something. Did they offer you a job?"

The wrinkles around Dad's eyes deepened, hinting at a smile. "They want me to head up their sales referral department."

"Head it up? Have you ever done anything like that before?"

"People adapt to survive, Nick. Part of the evolutionary process."

"It's straight commission," Mom said, still looking out the passenger window. "Your father is not taking the job."

"*I* haven't decided what *I'm* going to do, Sylvia."

Mom whipped her head around. "I've been in real estate long enough to know a scam when I see one, Frank, and that's what this job is. One huge rip-off."

"Lots of potential," Dad said to me, trying to sound upbeat. "And obviously they must think a lot of me; otherwise they wouldn't have paid to put us up in that nice condo. This is a hot area for retirees. I have a lot of connections in the Midwest. Kansas City, St. Louis, Des Moines. That's a market they're looking to penetrate."

"Scam," Mom repeated, almost spitting the word.

"So then you're thinking about it," I chimed in. "That's great. I'd love to live at the beach."

"*We* aren't living here because *your father* is not taking a job doing something he's completely unqualified to do. And don't think you're out of the woods, young man, not by a long shot. I haven't figured out what your punishment will be, but believe you me, by the time I'm done with you, you'll wish you'd never set foot in that boathouse."

I was tempted to point out again that it was Wendy who got into the canoe without a life jacket or paddle, but didn't. Once Mom gets her mean mask on, there's no use trying to reason with her.

"Sylvia, don't tell me what I will and will not do."

"You're not taking that job and we're not moving to Palmetto Island, and that's final."

Mom hated most everything about the coast of Georgia and took every opportunity to point out to my father that she wasn't about to move to a place overrun with flying cockroaches, mosquitoes, and alligators.

Dad shot back, "You want to pack up and move in permanent with your sister, go ahead, I'm not stopping you. Would be a relief not to have to listen to you complaining about how you can't afford to shop for new shoes—as if you need another pair."

"Frank, we both agreed we wouldn't argue in front of the kids."

"You started it."

I slumped in the Buick's back seat, resigned to the fact that my parents were splitting up. Thing is, I don't mind my parents not *always* getting along. That's normal. But saying bad stuff about each other in front of Wendy and me? It's like they don't even care how it makes the two of us feel. Or how hard it is for us to mentally referee their spats.

That's one reason I wanted Wendy to go with me to the boathouse. I was hoping the two of us could come up with a plan for how to keep our parents together. I knew for a fact Mom had contacted an attorney. Not sure about Dad. He's not one to give up easily. Not even on a lost cause. Not that our family was a lost cause, but it had definitely lost something.

Dad swung the Buick into an empty parking spot in front of our rental unit and turned off the motor. "I countered with a few conditions of my own. It's in their ballpark now."

As soon as we were inside, I bolted to the guest bathroom to shower. No matter how hard I tried, I couldn't get the smell of that stinking creek out of my nostrils. I also couldn't wash away the guilt. It was nagging at me, and I figured I wouldn't be able to get rid of it until I found my sister. Worst part was, no one would let me help with the search, and that was the pits.

When I came out, the canine unit was in Wendy's bedroom going through my sister's stuff. Shirts and jeans were on the bed, and shoes and socks lay strewn across the floor. A dog's furry head had buried itself in Wendy's favorite pullover hoodie.

Officer Latisha Hightower asked me to explain what happened. I told her about the *Cool Ghoul Gazette* and my involvement with TV Crime Watchers.

"What exactly is that?"

"The Crime Watchers? It's a group of us that analyzes crime, cop, and detective shows. We have a huge database going back almost thirty years. We use that information to catch real murderers. At least, when law enforcement officials will let us help. We have an 80 percent close rate. That means in most cases we can correctly identify the killer *before* the real detectives can."

"Interesting." I could tell from the way she said it that she didn't believe me. "Tell me about your sister floating away in the canoe."

I recounted how Wendy and I had taken the canoe from the rec center without permission, paddled out, and docked under the boathouse. How we'd waited for almost an hour and then Wendy got bored and wanted to leave. When I got to the part about seeing a dead person bobbing up and grabbing my sister, the nice police lady stopped taking notes.

"I'm sure you understand how important it is for us to get an accurate description of what happened," she said to me in a patronizing tone.

"That's what I'm doing, describing the thing that took my sister."

"You said it was foggy, right? Maybe you just *think* you saw a dead body."

"White dress, skin hanging off, head with a huge hole in the side. I got a real good look. It was a body, no doubt about it."

Officer Hightower turned toward my parents seated at the kitchen table. "Okay, I think we have enough to go on."

I could tell she didn't believe me. No surprise there. If I'd been a police officer, I would have had a hard time believing me, too.

The canine unit packed up their gear and dogs and left. Once the front door clicked shut, the condo became deathly quiet. Without saying good night, Mom shuffled off to Wendy's room. The door clicked shut. In a few minutes I heard her sobbing. I wanted to go in and give her a hug, but I was the last person she wanted to see, so I unfolded a sheet and sacked out on the living room sofa. Dad told me not to worry, that we'd find Wendy, and retreated to the master bedroom.

I lay there for a long time listening to a starfish wall clock click off the seconds. I couldn't sleep knowing Wendy was in that canoe with some zombie-like person. Hoax or not, my sister would be a basket case. The thing that had me stumped was why Wendy? If she had not crawled into that canoe, would the prankster have taken one of the teens at the bonfire? Or had my sister been targeted? Zombie festival or not, I couldn't imagine someone dressing up like that and swimming around in cold water just to play a joke on someone. I'd nearly frozen during my short time in the water.

Without meaning to, my mind replayed what I knew to be the basic profile of a kidnapping case.

From watching hundreds of TV shows and reading transcripts of real cases, I knew kidnappers normally target specific individuals. Only in rare instances is the abduction a random act. Most kidnappers either seek financial gain (victim held for ransom), have a political agenda (release of prisoners), or are emotionally and psychologically disturbed. It was that last category that concerned me the most. *What if a crazy goon took Wendy? Some freak who thinks he or she is a zombie and is acting out some fantasy?*

The good news was, in hostage-for-ransom cases, the victims tended to survive their ordeal. Bad news was, my family was broke. I wondered if our presence in the plush condo at Palmetto Island had given the kidnapper the wrong impression. If so, my sister could be in bigger trouble than any of us imagined.

The light in Dad's bedroom went off. A few moments later I heard him tiptoe into the kitchen and get a glass of water. The condo was so quiet I could hear Dad swallowing as he gulped water.

A few minutes later, I heard him quietly knocking on Wendy's bedroom door. Mom came out, sniffling. They huddled in the kitchen, the two of them talking in whispers. It reminded me of when I was younger and I would sneak out of my room and watch while they put out our Christmas presents. Finally Dad's car keys jingled, the front door opened, and light from the porch briefly fell across the living room carpet. Then it was quiet again.

I hated that Wendy was missing and I was to blame, but at least Mom and Dad were doing something together — even if it was only hanging out by the creek while awaiting an update from Officer McDonald.

Moonlight moved across the patio. The starfish clock ticked and ticked and ... ticked. Outside I heard the Buick start.

I lay there thinking about my sister. *Bet she's not sacked out on a sofa pretending to sleep. Bet she's bawling her eyes out and yelling for someone to come find her.*

Turning onto my side, I closed my eyes and wished I could take back the past couple of hours, but I couldn't. Wendy was gone, my parents upset, and for what? So I could write a stupid zombie story for *Cool Ghoul*.

I was still wide awake when soft knocking on the front door startled me. Jumping up, I went to the door and peeped out the little window. The girl from the creek, the one I'd seen wearing the faded denim shirt and jeans, was trotting across the parking lot, running away from our unit. I opened the door, looked down, and saw a note on the doormat.

> If you want to find your sister, meet me at First Union African Baptist in ten minutes.

The hum of an electric golf cart caught my ear and I jerked my head up just in time to see her speeding away up the darkened street.

In a kitchen drawer I found a small flashlight. It fit nicely into the front pocket of my jeans. I slipped on damp sneakers and grabbed my lightweight rain jacket. For a few seconds I stood in the living room wondering if I should leave my parents a message telling them where I was going, but decided against it. The more it looked like a spur-of-the-moment decision, the better.

I eased open the sliding glass door, mounted my bike, and pedaled across the alligator lagoon into blackness.

# CHAPTER FOUR
# A GRAVE DISCOVERY

The main route across the island was a wide two-lane road with a landscaped median decorated with palmetto trees and pampas grass. A lit rustic wooden sign at the entrance to the shopping area welcomed visitors to "Palmetto Island — A Southern Slice of Paradise." Pumping the pedals hard, I headed up the island, taking note of the expensive-looking homes with clever names like Bogey Nights, Caddie Shack, and Gopher the Greens. I knew Mom and Dad would be upset if they came back and found me gone, so I allowed myself one hour to find the First Union African Baptist Church, meet with the mysterious teen from the creek, and get back home.

When I reached the wildlife refuge center, I turned onto the sawdust path and headed into the woods. I came out on an elevated boardwalk spanning a marsh.

I love the smell of the wetlands. There's nothing like the broad sweep of marsh grass and the sour odor of low tide. I know Mom might not find the coast of Georgia appealing, but as far as I'm concerned, the beach music sound of waves lapping on sand beats the howl of winter's wind spitting snow any day.

The marquee sign in front of the church announced that Sunday morning's worship would begin at 11:00 a.m. This week's sermon by Reverend Patch Davis was titled "Buy a Vowel: Adding U to Ch rch."

I pedaled under a tunnel of oaks and propped my bike against the steps of the white two-story chapel. On one side was a small cemetery; on the other, wooden picnic tables spaced among oaks. A breeze lifted beards of moss from branches, bringing with it the smell of the sea and pine.

"Over here."

The girl from the creek sat on a swing beneath a tree. I wandered over. There remained enough moonlight shining through the branches for me to see she had sandy-blonde bangs, dimpled cheeks, and a long, slender neck.

"You know where my sister is?"

The girl pushed back and began swinging. "What were you doing in that boathouse?"

I jumped out of the way to keep from getting kicked. "Waiting for low tide. What about my sister?"

"That was dumb. That boathouse is abandoned for a reason."

"And you are not supposed to build a bonfire. I know because the rules are printed on a magnet that's stuck to our condo's fridge."

She shucked her flip-flops and leaned back, letting her hair trail behind. "Give me a push."

I stepped around and gave the swing a hard shove. "I'm sort of in a hurry here."

"You know about the Laveau girl, right?" She kept her head tilted back, revealing the creamy curve of her throat, and looked up at me with large opal eyes. "How she died?"

"Jumped from a riverboat like fifteen yeas ago is what I heard. I mentioned her accident in an article I'm writing. That's why I went to the creek tonight, to see if her ghost or body or whatever would show up again."

Before she could ask, I gave her a quick rundown of the *Cool Ghoul Gazette* and how I make money based on site traffic to my articles.

"Where you from?"

"Kansas."

"Well, Kansas, here's the thing you probably ought to know about the Laveau girl. After she died way back then, her parents tried to sue the riverboat company. She jumped, but her ma and pa claimed the crew was negligent for not keeping her from crawling over the railing. As part of their defense, the company's lawyers requested an autopsy. I'm guessing they were hoping to prove she'd been drinking or was on drugs. But when they dug her up and opened that casket, all they found was a whole lot of nothing."

"No way."

"Way. No bones, no body. Nothing. The judge declared a mistrial. Or maybe it never got that far. It happened around the time I was born. Thing is, up until this past Sunday morning, nobody'd seen Heidi May Laveau since the day she jumped from that riverboat." Suddenly she stopped swinging and shot to her feet. Tilting toward me, she said in a soft, almost whispering voice, "I heard you tell Officer McDonald a body floated up and grabbed the canoe. Was it her? Was it Laveau?" Her minty breath felt warm on my cheek. The way she asked the question, she sounded almost giddy.

"I don't know. I've never even seen a picture of her. Only know in a general way what she looks like based on the tip I received from the *Cool Ghoul* website. The officer who interviewed me suggested that maybe it was a publicity stunt tied to this weekend's zombie festival."

"How much do you know about voodoo?"

"Like black magic? Not much."

She slipped her feet back into the flip-flops. "Follow me, there's something I want to show you."

We left the large oak and headed toward the open field and cemetery. Given the number of stories we'd published on this topic in the *Cool Ghoul Gazette* website, it seemed possible, maybe even plausible, that there was such a thing as black magic. But I'd never heard of, much less witnessed, anyone putting a curse on another person.

We stopped beside a freshly dug grave. The moon's light shone on the nub of a marble base. I still couldn't figure out why she had me ride all the way up the island to talk to me about voodoo, black magic, and Heidi May Laveau. *My sister, that's what I want to know about. What do you know about my sister?*

"How much time you spent exploring the island, Kansas?"

"My real name's Nick. Nick Caden."

"Good for you. I'm Katrina, but everyone calls me Kat. You done anything fun other than sneak into that boathouse?" I told her my parents had kept my sister and me on a short leash since we'd arrived. "If you talk to the folks working in the hotels and club and such, listen to their stories. You'll find that a lot of them speak with an accent."

"Like yours."

"What're you talking about, an accent? This is how God talks." She jabbed a thumb toward a row of weathered head-stones. "That family right there? They're Gullah."

"Gull what?"

"Gullah; descendants of slaves. A good many of the blacks in this area still live in small farming villages and fishing communities. You end up going back to Kansas with a straw basket, chances are a Gullah person made it. They speak a sort of Jamaican, Creole dialect. This grave right here ..." She kicked a dirt clod into the hole. "It's for a housekeeper that worked at the resort's main hotel. Service is this Saturday. Her grand-daughter and I were best friends when I was little, but she moved awhile back. I might get to see her this weekend. Hang on, I need to check on something."

She trotted back toward the church and disappeared around the far corner.

While waiting for her to return, I studied the rectangular pit at my feet. Three feet wide or so, six deep. I could still see where the backhoe's tractor tires had left tread marks in the grass. In my mind's eye I pictured the bib of artificial turf placed around the pit. Folding chairs would be deployed, stainless steel poles erected to support a funeral-home tent for mourners.

It's funny how the imagination works, because in a split second, the picture morphed from a crowd of somber-faced men and women dressed in black to Mom and Dad standing alone beside a smooth polished steel casket. Wendy lay on her back with her hands folded one on top of the other. There was a slight smile on her face. In my mind I hadn't picked out her burial clothes. Maybe she'd wear her cheerleading uniform or the dress she and Mom had picked out for this year's Harvest Dance. The dress Dad hates because it shows too much of her neck and shoulders.

"Sorry, had to make sure it was still there."

The girl's comment brought my thoughts up from the grave.

"Where what was?"

"Forget it. You ever heard of a bokor priest? I'm guessing from that blank expression, your answer is no. A bokor is like a witch doctor, only worse. Zombies don't have a will of their own. They're like human robots, only dead. Most have a bokor that controls them."

"You brought me to a church to give me a lecture on zombies?"

"Helps to know what you're up against, Kansas. This ain't no Halloween dress-up party you're crashing. The thing that took your sister, if it's how you say it was, is a whole different sort of evil. The kind you ain't never seen before. Bet you've never been to Haiti, either?"

I shook my head.

"Some of us in church went on a mission trip there a couple of years ago. I didn't go myself, but the people in our group that went into the mountains came back talking about how the Haitians still practice voodoo. They sacrifice children, put curses on folks, and worship the devil. Some really sick stuff. Drinking blood and all."

"What's that got to do with Wendy?"

"Just making the point that every Halloween when kids dress up in scary costumes, what they're really doing is dabbling in black magic. Might not look like it. Might just look like an easy way to get free candy, but they're worshiping the king of darkness."

"They really sacrifice babies?"

"That's what they told me. A woman in our group actually

saw it happen. The reason I'm telling you all this is because back yonder that direction"—she paused, pointing past the church toward the water—"is Port Royal Sound. And beyond that nothing but creeks, snakes, gators, and miles and miles of swamp. You can't see it from here—can't hardly find the place till you're right on top of it—but in the middle of all that water is a Gullah lady who knows about zombies and voodoo. Find her and you can maybe find out what happened to your sister."

"And how exactly would I do that? I don't have a boat."

"That's what I ran off to check on. There's a skiff tied to the dock behind the church. The outboard can be hard to start, but once it's running you should have no trouble."

"If you think I'm taking a boat into a swamp to find a witch doctor, you're crazy."

"Gullah, not witch doctor. Big difference."

I peered into the yawning grave at my feet. "We are a long way from Haiti."

"Geographically speaking, yes, but culturally, it's like some of them never left. There's a mechanic at the marina that keeps a chicken coop out back of his trailer. He's Gullah. A few months ago, he got into a scrape with an employee at the golf club. Crazy mechanic went and killed one of his chickens and smeared blood all over the golf club employee's locker. Couple hours later, that golf course guy took sick and had to be hospitalized. Coincidence? Probably. My point is, a lot of what happens 'round here dudden add up. And when it don't, local folks swear it's 'cause someone put a hex on a body."

I liked listening to her talk. She had a funny way of making normal words like "doesn't" (dudden), "isn't" (iden), and "wasn't" (waden) sound interesting.

"Do you really think my sister was taken by a zombie? I mean, seriously?"

"You're asking the wrong question."

"Oh? What question should I be asking?"

"Who would want to take your sister? Think on that one. Now if it was me and my sister got snatched by someone dressed as a dead person, you can bet your bottom dollar I'd be doing everything I could to find her — including setting out to pay a call on Poke Salad Annie."

"Poke Sally who?" I asked.

"Annie. That's the Gullah woman I was telling you 'bout. She makes a voodoo gumbo that's to die for. Uses roadkill, water moccasin eggs, onion peels, rose thorns, shrimp, grits, rice, oysters, and bullfrog."

She pulled a crudely drawn map from her hip pocket and handed it to me. "Everything you need to know 'bout finding Annie's place is right there. Follow the map I drew and you shudden have any problem."

"How long will it take me to get to this Poke person's place?"

"From here? Ten minutes tops."

"I've only driven a boat one time and I almost hit the dock. Come with me."

"I might could have if it waden so late, but I'm past my

curfew. Uncle Phil will kill me if he catches me out this late. Keep a lookout for gators. Most times they won't bother you as long as you stay in the skiff. Check to be sure there's gas in the outboard. It has a fill tank on top. I shook the can. Sounded like it had plenty in it. Good luck."

She started toward her golf cart. I couldn't help but think of how much she reminded me of a girl I'd met last summer. Katrina didn't sound nearly as cultured or smart, but I'd gotten better at not judging people based on how they talked and dressed. In an odd way, I liked the fact that she called me Kansas. Made it sound like I was from someplace important, even though Kansas is about the most boring place there is.

She slid behind the wheel of the golf cart and pointed up at the Spanish moss. "Be careful going under branches with that skiff. If a cottonmouth snake falls on your head, that could be bad."

"Now you're just messing with me."

"See ya 'round, Kansas."

I watched her drive off. When the slipstream of dust disappeared, I shoved my hands in my pockets and walked around to the back of the church to see just what sort of shape this skiff was in.

## CHAPTER FIVE
# MY SISTER—DEAD TO THE WORLD

**I** found the flat-bottom boat, no problem. The people at the church were a trusting bunch. No padlock or chain. I checked the gas in the motor like she'd told me. Nearly full. Still, the idea of sneaking off the island, especially after what had happened to Wendy, left my stomach in knots. I wandered to the water's edge and looked west toward the smudge of light over the Savannah skyline.

So far, every move I'd made had brought nothing but trouble, and here I was thinking about sneaking off again without telling anyone. *But what if Kat's right? What if this Gullah person can help me find Wendy and I don't go? What's the worst case scenario?*

I let that question rattle around in my head. I didn't want to go there, didn't want to think about the answer to that one.

*She could die.*

I kicked sand with my sneaker and thought about my parents. Nobody had to tell me that losing a child was tough on a marriage. A boy in my school lost his sister to a drive-by shooting. It wrecked his family. His mom started drinking. His father got caught fooling around. The boy ended up in foster care until the judge could sort things out between his parents. By the end of the year it was like he had died, too.

I didn't want Mom and Dad to have to go through burying Wendy. Or me, for that matter. But at the same time, it didn't feel right leaving Palmetto Island without asking first. I pulled out my phone. Maybe if I called and explained to Dad what Kat told me, he would go with me.

Before I could pull up Dad's number from my contact list, an email message alert popped up on my screen. I swiped open my mail app and nearly dropped my phone when I got to the end of the first sentence.

Evening, Nick, look what I fished out of the creek.

Under the text was a picture of Wendy. She'd been blind-folded but still wore the Camp Kanata sweatshirt she'd put on before we left the condo. In the picture she appeared to be standing in a home or apartment or motel room. Behind her on the wall was a picture of a sailboat. The background was blurred, but it looked to be a small sailing dory.

> Too bad your sister had to leave suddenly. From the sound of things, you two were having a good brother/sister bonding time. I am sure she would have loved to hear all about your dad's bogus job offer and his big plans for moving to Palmetto Island.

What was meant by "bogus offer"? Had Mom been right? Was the sales job a scam?

> She is a fighter, your sister. I had a hard time getting her to settle down. But now she is . . . shall we say, dead to the world.

I scrolled down. As I did, I noticed my hands trembling.

> You may be wondering what I want. It's simple, really. I want my life back. And you are the only thing standing in my way.

> Do not try to trace this email. It would be a waste of time—time your sister does not have. And DO NOT show this to anyone. It would only make things worse for your sister. Yes, there ARE things worse than death.

> Enjoy the rest of your evening, Nick. I can assure you, your sister will not.

The email was signed Heidi.May.Laveau@coolghoul
gazette.com.

Feeling light-headed, I sat on the side of the boat. Obviously the return email address was bogus, since there was no
way my editor or anyone else on the staff would issue such
an account. But that didn't answer the question of *who* had
Wendy.

Certainly, someone who knew me, knew we'd come down
for Dad's job interview, and knew my parents were at dinner.
Had Wendy told the kidnapper all this? Had she been tortured? And what did the sender mean: *You are the only thing
standing in my way.* I didn't *know* anyone on Palmetto Island,
so how could I possibly cause problems for someone?

The email ended any thoughts I had about going to see the
Gullah woman. I needed to get back to the condo and make
a plan. One that involved backtracking every place I'd been
on the island and every person I'd met. Thing was, the only
person I had talked to for any length of time was the new girl,
Kat. Could she be the kidnapper?

I put my phone away and walked numbly back to my bike.
I did not remember the ride home or pulling into the parking
lot. I popped the curb in front of the condo and let out a huge
sigh of relief when I realized the Buick was still gone. I slipped
into the condo through the patio door, kicked off my sneakers,
and crashed on the couch. I thought about how scared Wendy
looked in the email, how her sweat shirt was streaked with
mud and her hair was damp. It was possible she'd fallen in. Or

maybe she'd jumped and tried to swim away. Either way, she was trapped now.

And it was my fault.

Closing my eyes, I sent Wendy a silent plea to hang in there. *Don't worry, sis. I'll find you, I promise. Just not tonight.*

# CHAPTER SIX
# PARENTAL GUIDANCE NOT ADVISED

It was still dark when I heard my parents come in. They tiptoed to the master bedroom and the door closed. I felt a little better knowing Mom was sleeping with Dad and not in Wendy's bed. That was a good sign, I hoped. Maybe my parents' dead marriage wasn't so dead after all.

The next morning I woke up to the smell of bacon frying. Rolling onto my side, I saw Dad seated at the kitchen bar with a legal pad by his elbow and a cup of coffee in his hand.

"Any luck finding Wendy?" The way he sat there making

notes, I wondered if maybe they had. *Could be she's in her bedroom snoozing.*

"They're still looking." My heart sank. "You sleep okay?" Dad asked.

"Caught a few winks." I couldn't tell if he was being serious or sarcastic. "How come you're not at the creek? Not waiting on me, I hope. 'Cause if you are, let's go."

"Fog," Dad said and made a notation on the yellow pad.

Mom came from the kitchen and placed a jug of orange juice on the table. "Breakfast is almost ready. Wash up."

After brushing my teeth and stuff, I dropped into a chair and speared a piece of bacon. "How long did you two stay at the creek?"

Dad shot Mom a look, then dabbed his mouth with a napkin. "We got back around two. By then the fog was so bad you couldn't see your feet. It's supposed to burn off, though. As soon as we're finished eating, we'll pack up, then head back down. We have to be checked out of here by eleven, anyway."

"But we're not leaving, are we? Not without Wendy?"

"We only had this place for the one night," Mom explained. "Your father has worked things out so we can stay an extra night someplace else, if necessary."

"Does Officer McDonald still think it's a prank?" I buttered a piece of toast and chugged the rest of my juice, then poured myself a second glass.

"General feeling is the canoe got swept upstream," said

Dad. "Might have floated into the Savannah River. They're widening the search area."

Out of the corner of my eye I saw my phone resting on the coffee table. I guess I stared at it too long, because Dad asked me if something was wrong.

"I ... don't think so, why?"

"You have that look, is all."

I felt my face grow hot. "What look?" I had a terrible poker face and it showed anytime someone called me out. That was one reason why I almost never lied to my parents.

"The look like the time you got after-school detention," Mom said sternly, "and weren't going to tell us."

"Did something happen after we left last night?" Dad asked.

"After you left?" I felt sick—run to the bathroom and hurl your breakfast sick.

Mom touched my elbow. "What *is it* you're not telling us?"

"I'm not ... I wasn't supposed ... Please, can we just drop it? I'm not supposed to say anything about it."

"Well, I think you'd better, young man."

I surrendered my phone to Dad. He put on his reading glasses and read until Wendy's picture came up. The blood drained from his face. Dad stared at the phone for several long seconds, then passed it to Mom.

With a catch in his voice, my father said to me, "And you weren't going to mention this?"

"You read it, you saw what it said."

With tears forming at the corners of her eyes, Mom cradled the phone as if it was a small stuffed animal. "I th ..." She paused, took a deep, shuddering breath, and, pushing the phone toward Dad, continued. "I think Officer McDonald needs to see this right away, don't you?"

"Should have had this hours ago," Dad seconded.

"But you see what it says," I protested. "I'm not supposed to show anyone that email."

"McDonald can probably figure out where it came from," Dad said to Mom. "I'll run this down to the creek while you two finish packing."

"I already tried. We have software up on the *Cool Ghoul* site that lets us map the route of an email packet. Calvin uses it when he's trying to figure out who's leaving nasty comments on the site. Right before I went to sleep last night, I ran a reverse lookup trace route. It showed that the email was sent from Kobuk Coffee on West 5th Avenue in Anchorage, Alaska."

"We'll let the police handle it from here," Mom said numbly. "They're trained for this sort of thing."

"I am, too, Mom. I've traced emails bunches of times. I'm telling you, whoever has Wendy isn't in Alaska. And they know we drove from Kansas to Palmetto Island, that you two were at a dinner meeting in Savannah last night, and wants us to believe he or she is connected in some way to Dad's job offer."

"Your mom's right. This is a matter for the police."

"Fine, but if you're going to show them that email, take my

tablet. I'll need my phone in case Wendy's kidnapper tries to reach me again."

"And if that happens, you'd better come to us pronto."

I gave Dad my tablet and showed him how to activate the email program, then asked, "What's next? Sleep in the Buick while we search for Wendy?"

Dad tucked my tablet under his arm, along with the legal pad on which he'd been jotting notes. "The realty company worked it out with the charter company so we could stay on a trawler. That's like a big, fancy boat. Made it sound real nice."

"Speaking of the realty company, how much do you know about the people you interviewed with?"

Mom paused in the middle of wiping down the table. "I was about to ask the same thing."

"You were at dinner, Sylvia. Did Ms. Bryant strike you as the type of woman who goes around snatching children?"

"These days, who can tell?"

I looked up at Dad. "Ms.?"

Mom said dryly, "Now you see why I insisted on going with your father. No telling what he might have said or done if I hadn't been with him."

Dad snatched his keys from the counter and left, slamming the door shut behind him.

Mom grabbed a sponge and began rinsing dishes. "Start gathering up your stuff. When you're finished, you can vacuum. After that we need to take our trash to the Dumpster."

"But isn't that what housekeeping is for?"

"Nick, would you please just do like I asked? I don't have the energy to argue with you *and* your father."

"Sure, Mom. Sorry."

"And regardless of what I think about Palmetto Island Realty and their supposed interest in your father, we can still act like we appreciate them letting us stay here. The condo was free, after all."

*Oh sure, it was free. As long as you don't include the cost of losing Wendy.*

# CHAPTER SEVEN
# A BIT OF MS. FORTUNE

When Dad had said we were moving onto a trawler, I pictured a shrimp boat.

Dad owns a copy of *Forrest Gump*. Actually, Dad owns every Tom Hanks movie ever made, including those early *Bosom Buddies* episodes starring Hanks and Peter Scolari. My favorite scene in *Gump* is where Forrest sees Lieutenant Dan on the dock and jumps from his boat into the water. But without a captain, the boat wanders off course and crashes into a dock.

That's what I thought we were getting—a Bubba Gump shrimp boat. But it turns out the word *trawler* is another way of saying big, honking, go-slow boat.

While Dad received instructions from a guy named Dan, Mom stood on the dock with her arms crossed. Judging from the scowl on her face, she was not impressed with our new accommodations. In fact, she looked like she was about to be seasick ... on land.

"Did Dad happen to mention anything about the email?" I asked. "Like, say, that the officer in charge found the person that sent it?"

"No. Only thing he said was that they took your tablet. Your father didn't come right out and say so, but he got the impression that Officer McDonald was pretty upset. If I were you, I would steer clear of him."

"That's fine. The way he's going about trying to find Wendy is a waste of time, anyway."

I stepped aboard, dropped Dad's bag on the deck, and looked back at Mom. "You want help getting aboard?"

She uncrossed her arms but didn't budge. "Bet you never knew that your grandfather owned a boat. Not this big, of course. It was more of a runabout. He wasted more money on that thing than he did on food, clothes, and farm fuel combined. My mom used to tell Molly and me that the only thing we needed to know about a boat was how to spell it: BOAT, B–O–A–T, or Break Out Another Thousand. 'That's how much it cost to get it fixed,' Mom would tell us. A thousand dollars."

"Dad sure seems to like this one," I said, hopping back on the dock.

"He would. My father would have, too."

For a moment I thought she might smile, but then her face returned to an uneasy grimace.

I strolled down the dock and noticed that our new home was named *Ms. Fortune. Not a good sign. Not a good sign at all.*

My father and Dan the boat man backed down steps and disappeared into the trawler. I grabbed Mom's suitcase and my duffel bag and stepped into the cockpit. That's what Dad had called it, a cockpit. I guess because the big space at the rear of the boat was large enough to hold chicken fights. I'd read in a Palmetto Island tourist magazine that cockfighting used to be popular in South Carolina and Georgia. Maybe it still was. I knew from billboards on the side of the interstate that the University of South Carolina called itself the Gamecocks, though personally I wouldn't be caught dead cheering for a team whose mascot is a chicken.

While I carried the rest of our stuff onto the trawler, Mom waited nervously on the dock. The boat was only a foot away, but from the way Mom eyed the chasm, you would have thought she was preparing to leap across the Grand Canyon. I'm sure part of her nervousness really did have to do with getting on the boat. If opposites attract, then my parents are a perfect match. The way Dad bounced on the balls of his feet when the boat man showed up, I could tell he was sky-high about being on the trawler. Mom, meanwhile, standing with her arms crossed, looked totally repulsed by the whole idea.

But she also looked tired. I could imagine that she hadn't slept much. There were bags under Mom's eyes and her mascara was smudged from where she'd been crying. I felt bad for her, especially since all this was my fault. But I'd said I was sorry a gazillion times and couldn't do anything more than that.

Except find Wendy, of course.

I stepped aboard and dropped my sister's luggage into the middle of the cockpit.

About the same time Dad poked his head out. "Oh, for the love of Pete, would you get on the boat, already?"

"Don't rush me, Frank. I'm trying not to fall in."

"You're not going to fall in. Couldn't if you tried. There's not enough space between the boat and dock for that."

"What are you saying, that I'm too fat? Is that what you're saying?"

"Here, Mom, take my hand. We'll go on three. One, two ..."

Mom let out a tiny squeak and tumbled aboard. "I don't know how I'm ever going to get off."

"You'll find a way, Mom, I know you will."

As soon as Dan the boat man left, Dad ordered us to "stow our gear." I wanted to tell him he sounded dorky but decided not to. I was already in enough trouble and I didn't want to give Dad another reason to ground me for the rest of my life. Fact was, without my sister around, I was about the only thing left holding my parents together. Maybe all kids feel this way when their parents aren't getting along, I don't know. But I had a sinking feeling that if I didn't do something to find Wendy, and fast, our family was doomed.

I helped Mom down the short ladder. We both paused at the bottom of the steps and looked around at the inside of the trawler. Dad started pointing at doors and drawers and closets and saying things like: "Aft cabin, forward state-room, head, bilge, engine room, salon, settee, nav station, galley, hanging locker." When he mentioned "hanging locker," my ears perked up. I looked to where he'd pointed and opened the tiny door. I couldn't imagine why anyone would call the small storage closet a "hanging locker"—especially since it was too small to strangle anything larger than a cat.

"Nick, I gotta check the water tanks. In the meantime, show your mom to the master state-room."

"The what?"

"Bedroom at the back of the boat. That's where the two of us will be sleeping."

*"Us." Well, that's a positive sign.*

I led Mom down a narrow hallway that forced us to walk hunched over. The back bedroom was actually pretty large. For a boat, that is. Mom did not appear impressed.

"How can your father possibly expect me to sleep in here?"

"Pretend we're camping. Only we're doing it on the water."

"But I hate camping."

"Then forget I mentioned camping."

After I showed Mom how to put her clothes in the tiny nooks beside the bed, we returned to the main part of the boat.

"Frank, can we go back to the creek now?"

"Sure. As soon as I show everyone how to use the head."

"The what?" I asked.

"Bathroom."

While Dad squeezed himself into a compartment the size of a broom closet, Mom and I gathered in the hallway.

Mom looked incredulous. *Incredulous* means unwilling or unable to believe something. For example, when the word appeared on my English exam, I was incredulous.

"Sink, shower, toilet," Dad announced. "Now watch carefully while I demonstrate how to flush."

"Frank, I really think we need to get back to the creek. What if they found Wendy and she's down there shivering cold and needing dry clothes?"

"Trust me, Sylvia, you *do not* want to be on this boat when the head backs up. This isn't like a house where you can grab a plunger and shove it down. If the toilet gets clogged, I'll have to remove those clamps down there, see?" Dad bent over and pointed like he'd repaired hundreds of marine toilets. "Then I'll have to pull the hoses. Don't need to tell you what is going to spill onto the floor when that happens. Now watch and learn. This will only take a few seconds."

Mom and I remained a safe distance away while Dad pumped a metal handle. He worked at it like he was auditioning for a job as a tire changer on a NASCAR Sprint Cup team.

"You want to make sure it goes all the way down," Dad said, sounding out of breath. "And even after it does, keep pumping. Otherwise some of it will float back into the bowl."

"Isn't there a button I can push?" Mom asked.

"On the newer models. But not this one."

I couldn't imagine Mom would ever use the boat's thimble-size toilet. Not when there was a perfectly good bathhouse at the end of the dock. The problem would be getting off the boat, but judging from her crinkled nose, I had a hunch Mom would find a way off . . . and probably stay off.

"Well, that about does it," Dad announced. "She's ready for the high seas. While you two get settled in, I'm going to change into shorts. Forecast calls for sunshine and temperatures in the seventies once this fog burns off."

"I'll wait for you on the dock," Mom announced. "Nick, give me a hand."

A few minutes later Dad came out wearing a floral-print shirt, tan shorts, and loafers without socks. He looked goofy, but I wasn't about to tell him.

Mom would take care of that.

"Your mom and I are heading back to the creek. I got the impression from Officer McDonald this morning that he's not keen on you hanging around. Can't imagine why unless he's already checked on you and found out how you can be when you think the authorities aren't doing their job. You are welcome to stay on the boat, hang around the marina and what-not, but please try not to break anything."

"Sure thing, Dad."

As soon as my parents were out of sight, I crawled onto the swivel seat in front of the steering wheel and gazed past the front of the boat at the sailboats and yachts parked in the marina. A stand of palmetto trees marked the shore's edge. Beyond the marina basin stood the faint outline of the boathouse perched over the creek. I spun the steering wheel and pondered what to do about Wendy.

I felt bad about what had happened. As Wendy's older brother, I was responsible for keeping her safe. She might not look at it that way. In fact, she hated it when I played the "big brother" card. But my parents had put me in charge and now she was gone.

I cataloged the possible suspects in Wendy's abduction.

*Heidi May Laveau. Real, live zombie? Doubtful. More like a real, live freak.*

*One of the kids from the campfire?* Kat was the only one I'd met, and she didn't strike me as a crazed kidnapper.

*Someone connected to Palmetto Island Realty? Ms. Bryant, maybe?* The email suggested the individual knew about Dad's dinner meeting. Maybe taking Wendy was a competing candidate's way of scaring us away.

I thought about Mom's comments regarding the reporters on the beach and Dad's warning to stay away from the creek. Could be the zombie abduction was part of a publicity stunt, but boy, was *that* risky. Taking a twelve-year-old girl, even as a stunt, could get you some serious prison time.

My phone buzzed. I checked the text message. It was from my editor, Calvin.

> Huge problems, bro. Site has been hacked! Don't try posting anything on the Cool Ghoul website, not even to comment on an article. I've revoked all IDs until we can figure out how this happened. Seriously, this is not funny.

Using my phone's browser, I pulled up the *Cool Ghoul Gazette*'s website. Sure enough, a blank page appeared where previously there had been headstone tabs with labels like "Breaking Noose," "Obits," and "Dead Lines."

As long as I had my browser opened, I checked our TV Crime Watchers site to see if I could find any shows where zombies kidnapped someone. A short list appeared with titles like *Skin of My Teeth* (show about an orthodontist who moonlights as a mortician), *Bare Bones* (survivalist family living in the Dakotas), *Dead Last* (a race car driver running a funeral parlor across from the Daytona Speedway). A synopsis of *Grave Discoveries* caught my eye.

> In the second season of *Grave Discoveries*, Jordon Gross investigates a series of kidnappings in Las Vegas, in which bookies with ties to the Campino family keep turning up dead in the trunks of cars, trash compactors and dangling from interstate bridges. In each case, witnesses claim a man fitting the description of a Las Vegas bookie was seen

fleeing the crime scene. Problem is, the police sketch of the potential killer matches a man Jordon knows. A man last seen dead on a slab in a Brooklyn morgue! To solve the case, Jordon infiltrates the voodoo world and meets up with a Mambo—a voodoo priestess. At her underground temple, Jordon learns that a mobster from a rival family has been systematically abducting and killing those who were scheduled to testify against him in a drug running case. Each time, the mobster poses as the dead Las Vegas bookie in order to conceal his true identity.

"Look at you, sitting behind the wheel like Captain Ron."

"Who?"

Kat rolled her eyes. Kat's unusual opal eyes looked beautiful even when they rolled.

"Any luck finding your sister?"

"Nope."

"Did you go see Annie like I suggested?"

"Nope, again." I swung myself from the seat and jumped onto the dock. "Good thing I didn't, too. My parents said the fog got so bad last night they called off the search. If I'd done like you suggested, I might still be out there, lost."

"If you want, I can run you out to her place. Won't take more'n a skinny minute."

"Better hang around here. My parents are pretty ticked about what happened last night."

"You mean ticked about meeting me at church?"

"They don't even know about that, thank goodness."

Kat removed her Palmetto Islands Marina ball cap and tossed back her sandy-blonde hair. "Smart move, Kansas. Don't want your parents to get the impression I'm a bad influence." Nudging me in the ribs, Kat added playfully, "If you're not careful, church can be habit-forming."

"Anyway, if I stay on the boat, I can still do research and try to figure out what exactly happened to my sister.

"Hey, how did you know where I was? You spying on me?"

"Like you're *that* cute. Oops, did I saw that out loud?" With mock embarrassment she hid her face behind the ball cap. Peeking above the bill of her cap, she winked at me, then said, "Uncle Phil. He's in charge of the charter fleet and I work at the marina. Help clean the boats and stuff. He told me we had a homeless family that needed a place to bunk down."

"I'm glad to hear someone finds our situation funny."

"Seriously, you need to go see Annie. She can help you find your sister."

"Yeah, whatever. Say, as long as you're here, I could use your advice. I'm doing a little research on my sister's abduction."

"Research?"

"One of my hobbies—actually, it's more like a job—is solving real murders by watching cop and detective shows."

"For real, you can do that?"

"Oh sure. Sometimes I have to watch a bunch of shows, but I can usually pick out the killer about halfway through each episode."

I handed her my phone and showed her the summary of

*Grave Discoveries*. She skimmed the synopsis and handed the phone back to me.

"So?"

"What I'm doing is looking for television shows centered around zombie abduction cases, or zombies that go around killing people. In every police procedure show, all the main suspects are revealed in the first ten minutes."

"All?"

"Yep. There are usually no more than three. Later in the show, a couple more suspects might be added or mentioned but they are never the killer. One character in the show is always the most obvious suspect. Usually they have a secret that forces them to withhold evidence. This makes the person look guilty. But they're never the killer. Same sort of thing happens in real murders. What I mean is, police will find someone who looks guilty, who has motive and means, and then the cops rush to build a case around them. But too often, that person didn't do it. There are lots of innocent people behind bars. Thousands, probably."

"So what exactly do you want to know?"

"Is it possible for someone who's into voodoo to put a curse on a person? I mean for real? I couldn't tell last night if you were messing with me or not, but if there is such a thing as black magic, I need to know. Might help explain what happened to my sister."

"Again, go see Annie. She's an expert on voodoo, black magic, curses, potions, and raising dead people from the grave."

I thought about that last part for a few seconds. *Raising dead people from the grave?* I wanted to ask how that was possible but I let it go. This girl Kat definitely had a different take on things. "Was there another reason you stopped by? I mean, other than being concerned about the homeless Cadens?"

"Oh, shucks, I totally forgot. You got a phone call. Come on, I'll walk you up to the marina."

On the way up the dock I said to Kat, "How come you're not in school?"

"I'm homeschooled. You?"

"Dad pulled us out for this trip. Called it an educational opportunity of a lifetime, which was basically Mom's way of saying Wendy and I couldn't be trusted to stay with Aunt Molly and Dad couldn't be trusted to come down here alone."

The Palmetto Island Yacht Club was a white, two-story building with rockers on the front porch and ferns in straw baskets hanging from rafters. From a thatched-roof café came the ping-pong sound of steel drum music.

Kat nodded toward the double screen doors. "Tell the cashier in the ship's store you have a phone call. When you're done, come find me and I'll put you to work."

I walked inside the ship's store and glanced around. Framed portraits of sailboats hung along one wall. Near the door stood a long bookcase filled with paperbacks and magazines. I waited for the woman behind the register to finish ringing up an older couple, then explained why I was there. She told me to go back out and wait on the porch by the pay phone, that she'd put the call through.

I picked up on the first ring. "Hello?"

In a husky feminine voice the caller said, "Morning, Nick. Is now a good time to talk? Your sister is dying to get this over with."

## CHAPTER EIGHT
# DYING TO GET SOME ANSWERS

**I** read that article you wrote about me on the *Cool Ghoul Gazette*." At the mention of the *Cool Ghoul* website I felt my stomach muscles tighten. "You have an interesting way of weaving facts into a story without making it seem dull. I especially liked the quotes you used from the fisherman."

*Probably using a voice modulation device,* I thought. *Or a smartphone app that alters the voice.*

"Should have been you in the canoe, not your sister. I thought it *was*."

"What do you want?"

"Who knows about the email?"

An older couple wandered onto the porch and parked themselves in rockers next to the pay phone. I shifted the phone to my other hand to create a barrier between us. In a hushed whisper I said, "Let me speak to my sister."

"The email, Caden, who did you show it to?"

The back of my neck felt prickly hot. Out of the corner of my eye I saw the man in the rocker leaning toward me as if listening.

"No one."

"We both know you're lying."

Droplets of perspiration tickled my ribs. With a slight quiver in my voice, I confessed. "My parents. They know about the email."

"And?"

"I ... they showed it to Officer McDonald."

"Bad move, Caden. Now I know you can't be trusted."

"Told you, it wasn't my idea. My parents made me."

"By the way, that reverse lookup trace route trick you tried? Not bad. Certainly a much better effort than what McDonald's people are doing."

A sour sickness settled in the pit of my stomach. "You have to believe me, I tried to do like you said, really I did."

"*I* don't have to do anything."

"Look, if it's money you want, my family doesn't have any."

"I already told you, I want my life back. And you're going to help me."

"If this is some kind of prank, you can—"

"No prank, Caden. I'm dead serious. Now then, let's see how serious you are about keeping your sister alive. Give me your log-in ID and password for that Crime Watchers database."

"Why? You going to crash that site, too?"

"What I do or don't do is none of your concern."

It occurred to me that only a few people on the island knew about my work with the TV Crime Watchers group: Kat, Officer McDonald, and the officer from the canine unit. Sharing my log-in with anyone was a huge risk. Not because of the database of TV shows. I doubted anybody cared about those. But because we'd paid a white-hat hacker to get us access to the National Crime Information Center—the FBI's database of all criminal records. Using my log-in information, someone could, theoretically, get into our system admin's directory and find the file.

"I ... can't."

"Oh, I think you can. ID and password—spit it out!"

"It's not that easy."

"You want me to hurt her, Caden? Is that what you want? 'Cause I will."

"Okay, okay, but first I need to talk to Wendy. I need to know she's okay."

"Not going to happen."

"Please, just let me talk to her. Then I'll give you my log-in information."

I needed to keep the caller on the line, needed to know how badly he or she wanted the Crime Watchers information.

There was an audible sigh on the other end, followed by, "Make it quick."

I strained to hear any background noises: footsteps, horns honking, a clock chiming, anything that might suggest Wendy's location. Only my sister's choking sobs interrupted the silence.

"Ni ... Nick." The laryngitis had turned Wendy's words into a raspy croak. "Please, Nick, just give h—"

"Wendy? Wendy!"

The old man spun in his chair and stared at me.

"Now you listen and you listen good, Caden. No more messing around."

"Put her back on, please."

"ID and password."

Haunted by my sister's broken voice, I cupped my hand over the speaker and betrayed the trust of my friends from the Crime Watchers site.

"Good boy. Mention this conversation to anyone and you'll never see your sister again, got it?"

Beads of cold sweat erupted on my forehead.

"Got it?"

A sickly wave of apprehension swept over me. "Yeah," I muttered. "I won't say a word." In the window's reflection I saw my parents coming up the sidewalk. Neither looked happy. I could imagine why. Obviously Wendy remained missing, but now, even though I knew how much danger she was in, I couldn't say anything to them. "So what's next? You want to meet someplace? Exchange Wendy for me?"

"Wave to your parents. I need to know that you know I'm watching your every move."

I threw my hand up, signaling to Mom and Dad that I'd be right there.

"Dusk. I'll find you at dusk. That's when the undead come alive. Enjoy the rest of your day, Caden. It might be your last."

# CHAPTER NINE
# THE TIDE WILL TELL

As I stood on the porch of the marina, the mallet sounds of steel drum music still beat out a festive tune, but the tenor of the day had hit a sour note. In the boatyard the modulated drone of a power washer dampened the *slap-slap* of ropes hitting sailboat masts. I pulled out my cell phone to send the Crime Watchers admin a quick message to let him know the site was about to be attacked, but first I needed to find out what, if anything, my parents learned about Wendy.

I shoved the phone back in my front pocket and joined Mom and Dad in front of a large sport fishing boat.

"Marine Patrol found Wendy's canoe in some reeds not far from here," Dad announced. "That's the good news."

I couldn't bear to look them in the face. The guilt of knowing Wendy was alive but being unable to share that news with my parents was killing me.

"She, ah . . ." My voice cracked under the pressure. I cleared my throat. "Is she okay?"

"Officer McDonald thinks her leaving in the canoe and you claiming a dead person took her might have been a ploy. He wonders if she snuck off to spend the night with friends. Tell the truth, Nick. Did you and Wendy plan all this?"

"What? No! It happened just like I told you."

Mom speared me with a glare. "See, Frank? Told you. He's incapable of telling the truth, even when caught in a lie."

"No, Mom, really. It happened just like I said."

Dad put his hand on my shoulder. "Officer McDonald also said you picked the lock and stole the canoe. Is that true, son?"

I studied the tops of my sneakers. I couldn't remember a time when I'd felt so bad. Wendy was in the hands of some deranged kidnapper dressed as a zombie who at that moment was doing who knew what to my sister. Worse, my parents had no idea how much trouble she was in.

I lifted my head and said as calmly as I could, "I wish you would believe me. Someone or something really *did* grab Wendy. We didn't plan any of this, honest. They have to keep looking for her — they just have to."

"Oh, they will," Dad replied. "Officer McDonald thinks they'll probably find her hanging out on the beach or in one of the boutiques. That's where kids on the island usually congregate during the day. They're checking the shopping center as we speak."

Mom turned to Dad. "Come on, Frank. Let's drive back to the condo and wait in the parking lot. Maybe if we're lucky, we'll spot her on the way."

"What do you want me to do?" I asked.

"What I want you to do is find your sister and tell her we're ready to leave," said Dad sternly. "And if it turns out that Officer McDonald is right, that you and Wendy hatched this scheme yourselves . . . well, we'll burn that bridge when we get to it."

"Cross that bridge," Mom corrected Dad.

"Let's go, Sylvia."

I watched my parents trudge toward the parking lot. As soon as they were out of sight, I sent the admin of our TV Crime Watchers group a text message.

> Just a heads-up to let you know our site might be hacked. I had to give someone my log-in info. If you can attach a worm to my account and follow it back, we may be able to find out who is behind the attack. Of course, you'll want to delete this text message as soon as you get it since the individual is probably monitoring my phone.

I sat on a dock box in front of the sport fishing boat and looked up at blue sky. Who on Palmetto Island knew about my hobby of solving murder cases? That was the big question now.

And how had the caller been able to ditch the canoe without anyone spotting him, her, or Wendy? Quickly I went down the list of everyone I'd met who knew I solved crimes by watching TV. It was a small registry.

Kat, Officer McDonald, and the canine officer. Officer McDonald had jumped on me pretty good for taking the canoe, but he didn't strike me as the sort who would go around kidnapping girls. Then again, the caller knew immediately that I'd shown the email to my parents and they, in turn, had shown it to Officer McDonald. To satisfy my own curiosity and perhaps cross a name off the suspect list, I decided to do some research.

Using my phone, I ran a quick web search of the words "cops" and "kidnapping." The results surprised me.

*Former Wichita police officer facing kidnapping charges…*

*D.C. police officer pleads not guilty to child abduction…*

*Ex-Moulton police officer charged with taking neighbor's daughter across state line…*

"Up for a picnic?"

Kat sauntered up the dock wearing a wide-brimmed straw hat and carrying a small cooler. "I got pimiento cheese sandwiches, cola, and we can split a Moon Pie for dessert. I'm betting you've never had one of those."

"Moon pie sounds like the sort of thing my Uncle Eric shovels out of the barn."

"Mercy me, Kansas. You ain't lived until you've shared a Moon Pie under a harvest moon while cruising down the

Savannah River. Stick around long enough, and I'll show you how to make Moon Pie pudding."

"Last night at the church, did you have your phone with you?"

She smiled mischievously. "If this is your way of asking for my number . . ."

"Ha-ha. Very funny." *Not a bad idea*, I thought. "Did you?"

"Yes, of course."

"Mind if I check something?"

I didn't really think Kat was behind my sister's kidnapping. At least I hoped not. I'd sort of become fond of her.

Kat's was an old flip-cover model. I scanned the sent text messages and instantly realized there was no way she could have sent me an email. At least, not from that phone.

"How much do you know about Officer McDonald?"

She put her phone away and parked the cooler beside the dock box. "Not much. Sometimes he and Uncle Phil will wet a hook together, but that's about it."

I scanned the marina parking lot. What I needed was a way to run down the few leads I'd come up with. None of them was very solid, but sitting around on a boat wasn't going to find my sister. "How far away is the Palmetto Island Realty office?"

"Clear on the other end of the island. But then, the island ain't that long. Why, your family thinking of buying a place?"

"I want to find out if Dad's job interview is legit. Mom seems to think my father is about to be conned into buying something we can't afford." I paused, thinking about how we couldn't afford *any* kind of home. At least not until Dad found steady work.

"I can take you up there in our golf cart if you like. It'll give me a chance to show you some of the funner things on Palmetto Island. Grab the cooler. We'll make our picnic a road trip."

As soon as we were out of the parking lot and on the road, Kat looked over at me. "You asked about Officer McDonald earlier. Don't know if this means anything or not, but one time he almost got written up for something that happened off-island."

The cooler sat between my feet. I'd looked for a seat belt and couldn't find one, so I clung to the roof support to keep from getting slung from the golf cart.

"Had something to do with this young country singer named Hank Cash. He was supposed to be promoting his new album, *Necking and Pecking on Papa's New Decking.*"

"Officer McDonald?"

"No, silly, Cash. Except right before Cash was supposed to go on the air, his manager phoned the station to say the singer was sick and cudden make it. The interview was a big deal for the station. They had been promoting it for weeks. So to keep from missing out on a big PR coup, the DJ that was supposed to be doing the interview dressed up like Cash, complete with wraparound sunglasses, cowboy hat, and boots. When the limo pulled up in front of the station, the DJ dressed as Cash jumped out and ran inside. The crowd went berserk and stormed the building. A seventeen-year-old girl got trampled during the process and nearly died."

"Hey, you know, I think I heard about that. Don't tell me Officer McDonald was the DJ?"

"No, but he was working off-duty and in charge of crowd control, so they blamed him for not keeping folks safe. Later it came out in the papers that Officer McDonald and the DJ were related. McDonald's cousin is the morning DJ at WSAV."

Traffic slowed. Kat stomped on the brake and the golf cart nearly slammed into the back of a black SUV loaded down with beach chairs and boogie boards.

"McDonald's cousin," I said. "Does he still work at the station?"

"Not sure. Maybe. How come you want to know?"

"Just thinking that if a zombie festival is set to start tonight and Officer McDonald is familiar with publicity pranks, he might be the perfect person to help his cousin dress up like a corpse and stage a mock kidnapping of my sister. At the creek last night he did mention something about the possibility of this being a radio station prank."

"Why not ask him? His office is close to the Realtor's office. I can drop you off if you want. Meantime, if'n you don't mind, pass me a sandwich. I'm so hungry I could eat a buttered monkey."

## CHAPTER TEN
# NIGHT OF THE LIVING DREADLOCKS

The golf cart trundled along behind a caravan of vehicles creeping up the island. I reached into the cooler and passed Kat her sandwich, then mentioned it seemed odd to see golf carts on the road with pickup trucks and SUVs.

"Actually it's the cars that are the problem," Kat explained. "Up until two years ago, golf carts and bikes were the only things allowed on the island. That bridge you came over on? It used to be a passenger ferry, but folks visiting whined about having to unload their stuff in a parking lot. Sissies. That's what a vacation is, different than home. So the town council ordered up an amendment to build the bridge. They kept the speed limit at twenty-five, though." She braked for an elderly woman with a walker entering the crosswalk. "I still say that if you want to find out what happened to your sister, you need to run and see Poke Salad Annie."

"Like a witch doctor is going to know where my sister is," I replied.

"Told you, Annie is a Gullah. Never claimed she was a witch doctor."

"What about that voodoo gumbo you told me she made?"

"That's just what she calls it. Don't mean she's into black magic. Besides which, you've eaten angel food cake, I bet. Does that make you an angel?"

"You don't really think there are such things as zombies, do you? I mean, seriously?"

"What I think dudden matter. You're the one who said a dead person took your sister."

The old woman cleared the crosswalk and we sped away.

Kat asked for a water bottle from the cooler. Between sips she said, "Folks in Haiti bury folks alive, did you know that?"

"Are we back to talking about zombies?"

"How it happens is like this. A bokor forces the victim to suck down this stuff called tetrodotoxin. It's a chemical found in puffer fish."

I knew what tetrodotoxin was, but I liked listening to Kat talk. She had a funny way of saying things.

"Even just a little bit can knock down the heart rate and make it look like the person has stopped breathing. It leaves a body feeling practically paralyzed. People who don't know any better think the person has up and died."

"Good thing I don't live in Haiti."

"After everyone skedaddles, the bokor sneaks back into the graveyard and digs up the body. 'Course they're not really dead, but the bokor makes like he's using magical powers to bring 'em back to life. Person coming through a thing like that is gonna do whatever a bokor asks, on account of they don't want to get planted a second time, know what I mean?"

"How do you know all this stuff?"

"I teach a weekly Bible study for recovering zombies."

I eyed her skeptically. "You're kidding, right?"

"Serious as a heart attack. Poke Salad Annie's in our group. That's how come I know about her voodoo gumbo. Sometimes she fixes a mess of it for us. If you're still around this weekend, drop by. Right now we're using *Undead: Revived, Resuscitated, and Reborn* as our study guide."

Kat thrust her left arm out, signaling a turn. As soon as the oncoming traffic cleared, we pulled into the real estate office parking lot.

*A Bible study for the undead. Unbelievable.*

Palmetto Island Realty overlooked the Atlantic Ocean on one side and a golf course on the other. A hedge of bushes provided a natural barrier between the parking pad and the shaded walkway. Kat parked the golf cart and I swung out.

"I'll wait for you."

"No need," I replied. "This might take a while."

"Got nothing else to do."

The rental office was on the ground floor of the two-story building. A sign by a wide staircase invited homebuyers to the second floor. When I reached the top step, the receptionist behind the mahogany desk looked up from her typing. I told her I was there to see Ms. Bryant, that my father was a candidate for a sales position and I thought I would visit their offices. Whoever sent the email of Wendy had suggested Dad's job offer was bogus. If so, then Ms. Bryant either was involved or might know who was behind it.

The receptionist studied me for a moment as if she couldn't believe a boy my age would check up on his father's work application. With a shrug, she gestured toward a waiting area of cushy chairs arranged in front of a large bay window overlooking a putting green. I wandered over and picked up a golf magazine.

In a few minutes a slender, twentysomething young man in a teal sport shirt and tan slacks came out of an office.

He introduced himself as Matthew Carter. "I understand you're here to see Ms. Bryant and don't have an appointment. I'm afraid she is busy showing a home. Is there something I can help you with?"

The way he said it made me think that helping me was the last thing Matthew Carter wanted to do. "Thanks, but I'll wait."

"She could be gone a long time."

"I'm in no hurry."

"How about you just give your name and number? I'll have her call you when she returns."

I seriously doubted Matthew Carter III, Senior Sales Consultant for Residential Development, as his name tag said, would pass along the message, but it was obvious the snotty sales assistant didn't want me hanging around. He jotted down my number and started back to his office.

"You ever heard of someone named Poke Salad Annie?" I asked.

He paused in the doorway of his office. "Oh, sure. Crazy cracker lives in the swamp. Why, you need a hex put on somebody?"

"Can she really do that?"

He tucked the piece of paper with my phone number into his pants pocket. "I'll see that Ms. Bryant gets the message." He retreated into his office and closed the door.

"That was quick," said Kat.

"Ms. Bryant is out with a client. I ended up leaving my number with her sales assistant."

"That would be Matt."

"You know him?"

"Matt caddied at the club for a spell. His granddaddy was one of the men who helped start Palmetto Island Resort. Did'n work at the club long, though. Golf pro kept getting complaints about Matt making improper comments toward the members, hitting on their wives and stuff. I might could've told them he was a bad seed, but nobody asked my opinion."

"So you two have a history, I take it."

"Oh yeah. He thinks he's the next heartthrob actor. Few years ago, Robert Redford was down here filming a golf movie. Matt got a bit role as an extra. All he had to do was stand in the crowd and keep quiet, but he couldn't even do that. He kept trying to steal the scene by spouting off one-liners while the actors were rehearsing. Finally he got booted. Next thing I hear he's up in Wilmington auditioning for a supporting role in a horror movie about some Rastafarians from Jamaica. *Night of the Living Dreadlocks*, I think it was called."

"Interesting. Did he get the part?"

"Didn't ask, don't want to know."

Kat reached over and placed the water bottle in the drink holder. I caught a whiff of sunscreen mixed with just a hint of perfume and for a split second my heart skipped a beat.

My sister once complained that I had a heart of stone, that I was uncaring and insensitive to the feelings of others. Feelings are overrated. Feelings get you into trouble. My parents' marriage was a good example. They'd fallen in love. Fallen—as if they didn't have a choice, like someone had pushed them. But they did have a choice and that choice had been clouded by feelings, feelings that faded. Now my parents were thinking about breaking up and splitting up Wendy and me. Nope, far as I was concerned, feelings were to be pushed down and ignored and only allowed outside when on a leash.

I'd become very good at burying mine.

"Where to now?" Kat was asking. "Officer McDonald's office?"

"Sure, if that's okay."

"Not a problem, but after I drop you off, I need to be getting back. The man renting the catamaran has phoned twice already to remind Uncle Phil that there'd better not be any problems. He's coming in and wants everything to be perfect. It's a boat, for crying out loud, not a Frisbee."

# CHAPTER ELEVEN
# CALL ME CONFUSED

Officer McDonald maintained his headquarters in the west wing of the town administrator's office. The men and women who hurried through the lobby were slender and fit and dressed in starched brown uniforms. No rubbery bellies or aimless loitering. An informational brochure in the newly carpeted lobby informed visitors that public safety and emergency response on Palmetto Island were handled through a contract with the Savannah Police Department. A framed picture on the wall showed a staff of seven uniformed men and women. Officer McDonald stood in the middle of the front row.

Behind the sliding glass door a woman spoke into a headset. She called codes for various types of emergencies. I waited while she jotted some words and numbers onto a notepad.

Television and movies have distorted our view of detective work. I know this because of my work with the Crime Watchers and the scores of interviews we've conducted with real men and women of the law. Less than 10 percent of investigative police work involves the examination of bodies, fingerprints, and blood. Most detectives spend their days filtering through seemingly trivial facts, chasing down leads through minor traffic violations, researching stupid complaints made by John and Jane Doe, and interviewing uncooperative witnesses who don't have a clue (and don't care) what real law enforcement officers do.

First responders on all levels are underappreciated, underpaid, and underfunded by the communities in which they serve.

And at that moment I felt a little like an underappreciated police detective. The search for my sister had reached a series of dead ends and nobody, not even my parents, cared. They thought Wendy was hanging out on the beach or at the food court with new friends, but I knew different. I knew she was in serious trouble.

First, the kidnapper had my email address. He or she could have lifted that off the *Cool Ghoul Gazette* website, sure. But how did the kidnapper know I worked for *Cool Ghoul*? For that matter, how could anyone on Palmetto Island have known my paying job involved writing articles for the *Gazette* and my real passion was solving murders by studying television episodes? It didn't make sense that a local would have known this.

Second, Heidi May Laveau's body floating up from the deep and grabbing Wendy was for show. Moviegoers may be infatuated with zombies and all things undead, but I knew decomposing corpses couldn't rise from the grave and go around taking people. So why Laveau's body? Kat knew more about the dear girl's background than anyone I'd met. But could Kat have known about my work with the *Cool Ghoul Gazette*? Maybe she researched me. After Wendy's abduction, Kat had easily tracked me down at the condo and lured me to the church. Had she been afraid I might go back to the creek with my parents? And if I had, was she worried I'd find the canoe, Wendy, and the person dressed up as Laveau? I had my phone. I could have called my parents and asked them to come back and pick me up. Maybe the church visit was Kat's way of covering for someone. But who?

The most troubling of all was the knowledge that whoever had Wendy seemed convinced that I could give them life. I could see someone taking Wendy for money, even revenge. But to demand something I couldn't deliver — that stumped me.

At last the receptionist looked up and slid open the glass. I explained who I was and asked if Officer McDonald was available. She instructed me to have a seat and went back to peck-peck-pecking on her keyboard. Whipping out my phone, I did a quick web search of Officer McDonald.

According to the bio on the Palmetto Island Law Enforcement website, Lieutenant Kevin J. McDonald joined the Savannah-Chatham Metro Police while serving as a Marine Diving Medical Technician stationed at Marine Corps Air Station in Beaufort, South Carolina. He left the Marine Corps with an honorable discharge after eight years of service and was hired as an officer. Upon graduation from the Criminal Justice Academy, he accepted a position as a patrol officer for the downtown precinct. Some months later he was promoted to the rank of corporal and assigned to the southside precinct as an assistant shift supervisor. Six months later, he assumed the rank of operations lieutenant of Palmetto Island.

The picture on the web page showed a younger-looking man with a buzz cut and fewer wrinkles around the eyes. The one item on his résumé that caught my attention was the diving certification. Whoever the individual was that had dressed up as Heidi May Laveau had been underwater a long time — maybe minutes — before snatching my sister.

A door opened. From the hallway an officer motioned for me to follow. Officer McDonald's office was in the back of the building. He sat behind a metal desk. Without looking up he waved me into a vacant chair and went back to signing a stack of forms.

His was a tiny office with metal file cabinets, beige carpeting, off-white walls, and a window looking onto a parking lot. The room smelled of aftershave and leather. I sat erect in the wooden chair and waited.

Officer McDonald put away his pen and pushed a button on the desk phone. Moments later the officer who had escorted me from the lobby entered the office, took the stack of forms, and left, pulling the door shut behind him.

"I only have a few minutes," Officer McDonald said to me. "What's on your mind?"

"Mom and Dad told me you're giving up the search for my sister. Mind if I ask why?"

"Not giving up, just changing the focus of the search. Did they mention we found the canoe?"

"Yeah, but that doesn't prove anything."

"Well, it proves your sister isn't with that canoe anymore."

"She's not out shopping with friends. I know that for a fact."

"Do you, now?"

"Yes, sir."

"Well, if it was me lost out there on Savage Island or some other place along that creek, I'd be yelling my fool head off."

"I thought you knew. My sister has laryngitis."

"Doesn't change the fact that there were no footprints anywhere along that creek bank." He stared blankly at me. "Last night you told me you and your sister rode down to the creek on bikes."

"Yeah, so?"

"Where's her bike now?"

I studied his face. The way he asked the question made me feel like *I* was a suspect in my sister's kidnapping. "I guess it's wherever your men hauled it to."

"Wrong. We never *found* any bike. Not at the creek, any-how. One of my officers did find one similar to the kind you were riding outside a townhome in the Turtle Dove Estates area. We checked the sticker. It's assigned to the unit your family was staying in. You want to know what I think? I think your sister slipped off and spent the night with some friends."

"We just got here yesterday; my sister hasn't had time to meet any friends. Besides, she's not like that."

He rocked back in his chair. "Was there anything else you wanted? I'm due to jump on a conference call in a few."

"What time did the call come in last night reporting my sister missing?"

"You know—you were there when your mom phoned it in."

"By the time my parents and I got to the creek, TV crews were already at the creek taking pictures of the boathouse. How did the wildlife patrol get a boat in the water that quickly unless someone called *before* Mom?"

Officer McDonald rubbed his chin and sighed. "The report on you was right."

"There's a report on me?"

He reached into a wire basket and pulled out a manila folder. Flipping it open, he lifted a sheet and held it up for me to see. "Says here you helped solve a murder in North Carolina some months back."

"Yeah, so, what of it?"

"Officer in charge of the case called you, and I quote,

'arrogant and pushy. Boy acted like he knew better than me how to investigate a murder,' unquote."

"The victim was dressed like a vampire. Someone had stabbed him in the chest with a wooden stake. No one in charge acted like that was odd. I thought it might be a good idea to find out who the murderer was."

"And you did that, how? By watching TV?"

"Something like that," I mumbled.

He riffled through the folder and scanned another document. "Before the North Carolina case you accused a federal marshal in Colorado of murder."

"He wasn't a federal marshal, just the marshal of a ghost town. I found the actor playing the role of Billy the Kid dead in the hayloft. They told me I was mistaken, that it was part of the 'ghost town' experience. I did some digging. The marshal in Deadwood Canyon had motive, means, and opportunity, so I questioned him. Statistics show that law enforcement officers commit roughly the same number of violent crimes as the general population."

"I wouldn't be too quick to lump me into that group. You don't want to get on my bad side."

I shifted uncomfortably in my chair. I had a hunch Officer McDonald didn't care much for me and had only agreed to the meeting to keep my parents happy. Their daughter was missing and it was his job to find her. If I had questions or concerns, I imagined Officer McDonald felt obligated to entertain those questions, even if he did view me as a nuisance.

"Can you check to see if someone else called 911 before Mom did?" I asked. "Is that possible?"

Ignoring the question, he kept reading. "Says here in the murder of Bill Bell, you bungled the investigation. Messed things up so badly that the trial judge threatened to postpone the case until a hearing could be held concerning the circumstances surrounding the suspect's arrest."

"The man shot two people. I got a taped confession. How's that not grounds for a murder charge?"

"Innocent until proven guilty. Just because *you* say he shot two men and *you* secured a taped confession doesn't make it so. This wouldn't be the first time an innocent man was wrongly accused. Not that it matters much now."

"Well, it sure does matter."

His face bunched into a scowl of concern. Leaning forward, he rested his elbows on the desk. "Thought you knew. From the way you acted last night at the creek, I thought you knew everything."

"Knew what?"

"The judge set bail at half a million dollars and released the deputy, Patrick Gabrovski, pending a thorough investigation into the circumstances surrounding his arrest. A few weeks later, Gabrovski was involved in a fatal traffic accident."

"He's dead?"

"Went off the road at a high rate of speed and slammed into a bridge abutment. Truck caught fire. They identified him from dental records."

Suddenly a coldness gripped my heart. Gabrovski's case was the first I'd cracked using our Crime Watchers formula, and the editor at *Cool Ghoul* had hired me primarily for my detective work in Deadwood Canyon. Calvin had made it clear that when Gabrovski's case went to court I would be featured on the home page of the website and maybe even sent back to report on the trial. Now Gabrovski was dead. In a strange way, I felt responsible. If I hadn't been so eager to secretly coax a confession out of him, I never would have messed with the case and he might be sitting in jail still awaiting trial.

Trying not to sound too disappointed, I said, "What does any of this have to do with you finding my sister?"

"Just this. We're doing all we can to find your sister, same as we would for anybody else. And what we don't need right now is you playing detective and making a mess of things ... like you did in Deadwood Canyon. That's why I asked your parents to keep you away from the creek, the reporters, or anyone else involved with your sister's search."

Officer McDonald picked up the phone. He punched a button and asked to have the emergency call log brought to him.

He hung up and said to me, "Anything else I can do for you?"

I wasn't sure if I should push the issue. The conversation definitely had not gone as I'd hoped. "Your cousin, does he still work at WSAV?"

McDonald's eyebrows arched. "Come again?"

"I know your cousin is or did work as the radio host at the station. I also know about what happened with the Hank Cash interview."

The corners of McDonald's eyes twitched. I'd seen the same irritated look from the marshal in Deadwood Canyon and the officer in Transylvania, North Carolina.

"What's your point?" McDonald asked.

"I've been thinking that if your cousin really wanted to improve the ratings for his show, planting a make-believe dead body on Palmetto Island the week before Savannah's big zombie festival would create a lot of buzz."

His neck muscles swelled. "Careful, son. You're real close to getting tossed out of this office."

"And wouldn't it be convenient if someone posing as a zombie snatched a body the night before the event was to start? Something like that would make news, I'm sure. You know, get people talking about the event who had never heard about a zombie festival? You were in the military, right? As a Marine Diving Medical Technician? Did you have anything to do with my sister's abduction?"

"Now you've stepped *way* over the line. If it wasn't for the fact that—"

A knock on the door cut him off before he could finish. The same officer as before stepped in, placed a call sheet on the desk, and left.

Officer McDonald scanned the report and grunted. "Guess you were right." He placed the readout on the desk and turned it so I could read. "Emergency operator received two calls about your sister last night." He tapped the paper. "First one came in six minutes *before* your mother phoned."

I studied the readout. "Hey, that's my cell number!"

"Is it, now?" Officer McDonald leaned across the desk and said sternly, "What sort of stunt you trying to pull, young man, coming in here accusing me of having something to do with your sister's disappearance when you know good and well *you* were the one who phoned it in?"

"Wha ... Hang on, that wasn't me! I didn't even have my phone on me. It was in my backpack—the backpack *you* gave me when I got back to the beach."

"Know what I think?" McDonald leaned back in his chair and locked his hands behind his head. "I think you and your sister planned this whole thing from the get-go. I think she snuck off to meet some kids and asked you to cover for her. You took a canoe from the rec center, shoved it out in the creek, and then called to make it look like she'd gone missing. Soon as she was away, you hurried back to the condo to meet your parents."

"But if I was going to do all that, why would I leave my backpack in the boathouse?"

"Because you're only a kid and not smart enough to know better. Tell you what I'll do. For now I won't charge you with making a false emergency call. I'll wait until I have more information. But you'd better believe if it turns out you made up this story about your sister, I *will* file charges."

I fought to keep my legs from trembling, that's how mad

I was. *Me? You think I'm the one behind this? How about you tell me where you were last night when my sister was abducted. Tell me that, Corporal Kevin J. McDonald!* I didn't say this, of course. The fact that my phone made the first call pretty much meant McDonald would never believe Wendy and I hadn't planned the whole thing.

Unless he was behind her kidnapping. Then he would know I was telling the truth.

Flustered, I blurted out, "Who did you interview last night besides me?"

"Just you, those teens at the bonfire, and that girl you saw me talking to. She's the one who suggested I check the boathouse. Good thing I did, too. Otherwise, I wouldn't have found your backpack." He stood. "Now, I need to get on that conference call."

I remained seated. "Last night you pointed to someone standing by the cart path. You said it was the manager of the activities center. Any idea what time *he* arrived at the creek?"

"Just after you did. You want to interview him, be my guest. He's in the building. I can get him for you, if you want."

"That'd be great."

Officer McDonald went out without closing the door and left me alone in the office to sort out facts surrounding my sister's disappearance.

Talk about being confused. It didn't make sense that someone would sneak back into the boathouse to use my phone to report her abduction unless ... unless someone *knew* Wendy and I would be in that boathouse. But who? I thought about the anonymous comment posted on the *Cool Ghoul* website, the one that first alerted me to the mysterious appearance of Laveau's body. It was that posting that had lured me to the boathouse. *But why would someone want me to be at the creek during low tide?* The answer came to me and it chilled my blood. "Should have been you in the canoe," the caller had said. "Thought it was."

I'd been set up from the get-go.

And I was still being played.

McDonald returned and introduced me to a young man with shoulder-length black hair and a stubble beard.

"Dirk, meet Nick Caden. Nick's sister is the girl who went missing."

I stood and we shook hands. Dirk had a lanky frame and broad shoulders. He was a good six inches taller than me, with an amiable manner about him.

Tossing back shaggy bangs, he looked at me with chlorine-blue eyes and flashed a big smile. "Officer McDonald said you wanted to chat, but now isn't good for me. We're both getting ready to go into a meeting. Can we meet in, say, an hour in the parking lot of the main beach access?"

"Yeah, I guess, but how do I get there? I don't have a ride."

"A shuttle can drop you off."

Before I could find out where the shuttle stop was, both men slipped into the conference room across from Officer McDonald's office. As the door was beginning to shut behind them, I saw Officer McDonald lean over and whisper something. Dirk looked back quickly and the door closed, leaving me to wonder if I'd gotten too close to the truth and was about to become the second Caden to go missing on Palmetto Island.

# CHAPTER TWELVE
# DUNE OUR THING

Standing in the shade of the shuttle bus stop, I checked my cell. I'd turned off the volume for my meeting with Officer McDonald, but now a text message from Ms. Bryant let me know she was on her way to a home on the beach called "Dune Our Thing." If I wanted to chat, we could meet there.

At a quarter after one the shuttle dropped me off in front of a three-story home with silver-gray cedar siding. A white wooden sign mounted by the mailbox asked that visitors respect the privacy of the owners and avoid using the private beach walkway. No cars in the drive. The front lawn of carpeted Bermuda grass needed cutting and a row of bushes trimming, but otherwise the place looked immaculate. I approached the home and peeked through a downstairs window that looked into the garage. An assortment of beach toys hung from the ceiling and walls: kiteboards and Windsurfers and kayaks.

Ignoring the privacy warning, I followed the wooden walkway around the corner of the house and up the dunes. I took a seat under the gazebo to await Ms. Bryant's arrival. A short ways up the beach a young father unlimbered a blue umbrella and began spreading towels. Two small boys emerged from the dunes dragging boogie boards across the sand. Some distance behind, the mom followed carrying an infant in her arms. *A nice young family enjoying their vacation—sort of like the way we used to.*

Small, brown-green swells slapped the sand. Birds with toothpick-thin legs skittered away from the surf rushing up the sand.

I thought about what had happened to Wendy and the *Cool Ghoul* website and tried to make sense of it. I wondered why someone would want to snatch me from a canoe at dead low tide. When the puzzle appears out of focus, the thing to do is sort the pieces into piles.

Officer McDonald was one piece. At first he'd been eager to find my sister, but not anymore. The way he'd lunged at the notion that I was the first one to call the emergency operator suggested he was eager—maybe too eager—to pin the blame for Wendy's disappearance on me. Which got me to wondering what I'd find if I looked in the trunk of his cruiser. A wet suit, maybe? Perhaps a sodden party dress, rubber skin, and fake blood?

McDonald's cousin was another mystery piece. Given the growth of radio services like Sirius and XM, along with Internet-streaming apps like Pandora and Rhapsody, I imagined maintaining a steady listenership for conventional radio would be difficult, especially with kids my age. What better way to grab the younger audience than to make it appear that a zombie had abducted a young teen? And who better to carry out such a stunt than a struggling actor with a bit part in a slasher movie? I made a mental note to circle back and find out if Matt Carter and McDonald's cousin knew each other.

Kat was another odd fit. She seemed nice enough, but why the pressure for me to meet Poke Salad Annie? Were the two working together? Had Kat grabbed Wendy and passed her off to the Gullah gal? And if so, why?

My parents were perhaps the oddest piece of all. They had been determined to keep bugging Officer McDonald until he found my sister, but now both seemed resigned to the fact that their youngest child had simply slipped off to spend the night with friends. It occurred to me that I might not be the only one getting mysterious messages. Maybe Mom and Dad had been warned to back off, too.

With the swipe of my thumb I unlocked my phone and brought up the TV Crime Watchers home page. Maybe if I could dig deeper into the zombie episodes I'd reviewed earlier, I could get a better idea of who was behind my sister's disappearance. Instead of the normal log-in screen, a large headline appeared on the home page warning visitors that they'd just downloaded a virus. Quickly I powered off my phone.

"You the young man who stopped by my office earlier?"

Startled, I looked over my shoulder. The middle-aged woman wore dark blue slacks, a gold belt, and a white blouse with a gold cross hanging from her neck. With each step, glossy blonde bangs bounced. Her face, arms and hands were tanned to the color of butterscotch. She was attractive in the way businesswomen can be when they are confident and successful. I knew the type. Mom had projected that same look when she'd sold real estate in Lawrence.

She offered her hand. "Liz Bryant."

Ms. Bryant's grip was strong and soft. I introduced myself as Frank Caden's son.

"Caden, Caden, don't tell me, it'll come to me."

She closed her eyes and pressed a knuckle to her golden-brown forehead. Shiny rings adorned fingers on both hands.

"Three-bedroom townhouse on Turtle Dove Lane. The one with a view of the eighth hole. You are the young man we hired to haul off those limbs and other debris, am I right?"

"Um, no. You had dinner with my parents last night, in Savannah."

"Oh, *that* Frank Caden. Sorry, I have my sales hat on. This place is coming back on the market and I was thinking about all the landscaping and yard work that needs to be done."

I looked around at the dunes, sea oats, and sand. "But it's on a beach — who cares what the yard looks like?"

"Honey child, you have no idea. People who buy homes in this price range care about *everything*. If you want, I'll show you around. I have to check on a few things, anyway."

"I doubt my parents would ever be able to afford something like this."

*Right now we can't even afford to buy a refrigerator box to sleep in.*

"Never hurts to dream." She waved in the direction of the three-story home, adding, "And beach dreams are the best kind."

I waited in the shade of the front porch while she slipped a key into the lock. She bumped open the door and a blast of cool air assaulted us. I followed her into a large open room that was at least twice the size of the whole downstairs in our old home in Lawrence.

"What was it you wanted to talk to me about?"

"My dad. I was wondering, is he a serious candidate for the sales job?"

"Absolutely. Why?"

"Mom thinks it's all a scam, that you only brought us down here to trick us into buying property on Palmetto Island."

Ms. Bryant put her purse on the kitchen counter and faced me. "I mean this in the nicest way possible, but your parents couldn't afford the rental deposit on the unit you stayed in." She must've seen my cheeks redden because she quickly added,

"Oh, don't think I was being nosy. But I had to run a full background check on your father before I contacted him about the position. We can't afford to invest this kind of time and effort in a candidate without vetting them first. Here, let me show you the kitchen. Your mother would die to have a kitchen this size."

The backsplash tiles were light beige with a scalloped seashells design. Recessed lighting under the cabinets reflected off black granite countertops. Hardwood floors, polished smooth, reflected the light streaming in from the floor-to-ceiling front windows. Ms. Bryant opened a double-door stand-up freezer that looked as if it belonged in a restaurant.

"Let me take you upstairs to the man cave. If you and your dad like watching sports, you'll never need to go to another live event again."

I followed her up the staircase. "Why Dad? I mean, he's spent his whole life revamping assembly lines."

"That's precisely what makes him the ideal candidate. He understands the importance of the process and execution. If you give your father our sales manual, what's he going to do with it?"

"Read it, highlight it, study it."

"Exactly. I bet in a month he would be able to recite the whole manual word for word. Men like your father are not rare, but they are special. I hate to use the phrase 'old school,' but that's what he is. He learns things from the ground up. With your father, there are no shortcuts, am I right?"

"Oh, he's by the book, that's for sure. Especially when it comes to school. Once I had this Language Arts teacher, Mrs. Harris. She was a nice woman who had absolutely no business being in a classroom. When she wasn't looking we'd throw paper airplanes across the room. Everyone in the class made As but that's because we were cheating on her tests. Come January, after our Christmas break, we found out Mrs. Harris had suffered a nervous breakdown. They gave us a sub but everyone still ended up making pretty good grades. After the school year was over, Dad found out I'd cheated and he went and told my guidance counselor. She said since the grades had already posted she couldn't change them, but I did start the next year with detention. So yeah, Dad's a stickler for the rules. Except when he's driving. Then the rules don't apply to him."

At the top of the stairs we turned down a hallway. She showed me bedrooms, bathrooms, and a master suite nearly the size of the condo we'd stayed in.

"You met my assistant," said Ms. Bryant. "What was your impression of him?"

"Thought he was rude and stuck up."

"Most clients think so, too. He's been with me almost three months and still doesn't know the first thing about customer interfacing. If I put your father in that job, he'd be the most upbeat, engaging salesperson you'd want to meet, am I right?"

"So long as he's not in rush-hour traffic, yes."

"A go-getter like your father is just the sort of person I need working for me."

"So the job offer is for real?"

"It's listed with professional recruiters and on all the major job search websites. That's how legit it is." We'd stopped outside a door at the end of the hallway. "Ready?" She pushed open a bright red door.

The man cave looked like a miniature sports bar. Monitors covered the front and side walls. Trophy cases filled with sports memorabilia stood on either side of the door. Banners from the SEC universities hung from the ceiling and hand towels of NFL teams lay draped across armrests. An angry-looking rooster was stitched into crimson carpet, indicating that the homeowner was a University of South Carolina Gamecocks fan.

"There are thirteen monitors," boasted Ms. Bryant, "with another three on the upper deck for night games under the stars. The room seats fifty. Last February, the owner had more than two hundred people over to watch the Super Bowl." Turning toward me, she motioned toward the monitors and chairs. "So what do you think? Does this give you any ideas? Make you want to dream?"

"Thing is, I'm not really into sports. Except for the X Games. Those I like. I'm more into skateboarding. But I could see where having all these monitors tied to close-circuit video feeds of certain high-crime areas would be helpful. I could sit in one of those chairs and actually watch detectives investigate crime scenes."

Ms. Bryant's smile dipped momentarily. Regaining her bubbly enthusiasm, she directed me back into the hall. "Let me show you the Cinderella room! You have a sister, right? Couple of years younger?"

"Actually, that's sort of what I wanted to talk to you about. By any chance, did you mention anything to anyone about my dad coming down here? Like, maybe your assistant?"

"Heavens, no. If Matt had any idea we were interviewing candidates for his position, he would become totally impossible to work with."

"If he's so bad, why haven't you fired him already?"

"I believe in giving people second and third chances. Matt is on his fourth. Once we get the new hire in place, I'll move Matt into some other role where he doesn't have to interact with clients."

We'd stopped at the top of the staircase. I looked at the open room below the banister and imagined what it might be like to live in a palace at the beach.

"The job is straight commission, but your father didn't seem bothered by this. In fact, I think he took it as a challenge. Whoever we put in that role will need to hit the ground running and work hard and fast." She paused and looked me up and down. "I must say, I've never had a family member of a prospective employee interview *me* before. It's a little off-putting."

"I care about Dad's job, sure, but the real reason I wanted to chat is because of my sister. She went missing last night while my parents were having dinner with you. I'm trying to figure out who might have known the two of us would be home alone."

"Oh my gosh, I had no idea that was ..."

"Thing is, I'm pretty sure someone knew Dad was coming down for the job interview."

Instantly her bubbly personality switched into one of concern. "Come out to my car. There's something you need to see."

I followed her around the house while she turned faucets on and off, flushed toilets, and replaced burned-out light bulbs. In the downstairs guest bath she added toilet paper and filled a hand soap dispenser. Back in the driveway, she unlocked the passenger door and thumbed open the glove box.

"This arrived in the mail last week." She handed me an envelope. "It is addressed to the director of sales and marketing. At first I thought it was a job application, so I tossed it in the basket with the others. But when I finally got around to looking at it, I realized it was a letter of recommendation for your father. You said you thought someone knew your family was coming to Palmetto Island. This might help you figure out who that someone was."

To whom it may concern,

Mr. Caden has asked me to write a letter in support of his application for employment with your firm. To be honest, I am dumbfounded. Not only am I astonished that he has the nerve to ask me to write such a letter, but also that he would seriously consider going into sales.

I met Mr. Caden some months back. He distinguished himself by rarely appearing attentive or interested in the people around him. As a consultant at our manufacturing plant, he was obnoxious and unreliable and completely overwhelmed by the intricacies of our assembly line. On those rare occasions when I permitted him to actually work alone, his performance was marred by mistakes, excuses, and blame cast upon others.

I can think of no one less qualified for real estate sales work than Frank Caden. I suggest you toss his application in the trash.

Sincerely,
K.G.B. Savior

"Wow, someone really hates my dad's guts."

"Quite the opposite. Whoever wrote this *wanted* me to interview your father."

"They did?"

"Oh, absolutely. After receiving a letter like that, I *had* to meet your father — if for no other reason than to satisfy my curiosity. In all my years of screening applicants, I have never seen a letter that set the expectations so low. At dinner last night, the only thing your father had to do was say hello and not talk with food in his mouth and I would have been impressed. Look at where the letter came from."

I studied the envelope. "Hey, that's *our* zip code." I peeked inside the envelope to see if there was a business card or any other clue, but it appeared empty. "Would it be okay if I hung on to this?"

"Be my guest." She held open the passenger door. "Can I give you a lift somewhere? I'm heading back to the office."

"I'm supposed to meet someone at the main beach access. Is that far from here?"

"Too far to walk. Hop in."

We pulled onto the road and headed toward a water tower painted to look like a giant golf ball on a tee. For the life of me, I could not think of anyone back home smart enough or creative enough to compose a letter like that, but it confirmed my hunch that the author of the email had orchestrated our family trip to Palmetto Island. And if so, then maybe my sister's abduction wasn't a random act or a publicity stunt, but a carefully planned act—one designed to terrorize my family.

While waiting for a pair of golf carts to cross the street, Ms. Bryant said, "Earlier you mentioned something about Officer McDonald thinking your sister is with friends. But the way you said it, I got the impression you don't believe him."

"I know for a fact that's not what happened. I just can't seem to convince him of that."

"You know, that's not surprising. Officer McDonald can be pretty headstrong. In fact, I'm somewhat surprised he is still working here."

"Why's that?"

"Palmetto Island can be an expensive place to live. Especially for someone in the service sector. Most of the island's labor force lives off-island and commutes, but not Officer McDonald. His home isn't lavish: a two-bedroom cottage in a cluster community. But it's not cheap, either. That may be part of why he's behind on mortgage payments."

"How would you know that?"

"He made an offer on a townhouse a few months ago. Told me he wanted to get into passive real estate investments—you know, rental property. We ran a credit check. I suggested he get current with his mortgage company, clean up his record, and try again in six months. And I hinted he might want to sell his condo and move off-island. He nearly bit my head off at that suggestion. He must've found another Realtor willing to work with him because somehow he got approved for the loan. But unless his finances have changed, I cannot imagine he's able to make two mortgage payments."

"Maybe someone cosigned the loan. Mom says that happens all the time."

"Possibly. His cousin is a hotshot radio host over at WSAV. He might have come into the deal. Even so, I still would not have been comfortable selling Officer McDonald that town-home. An officer under financial stress can be tempted to do some pretty shady things."

We turned into a beach access parking area and she nosed the Jag into an empty slot.

"Thanks for the ride." I stepped from the Jaguar and started to close the door, but stopped. "Mind if I ask why you kept that letter of recommendation?"

"No reason, really. Just a hunch." I noticed her fingering the cross on her necklace. "Sometimes I get a sense that I'm supposed to do, or not do, something. A lot of times if I pay attention to that gentle nudging, I find out later there was a divine purpose behind it." She smiled warmly at me. "Good luck finding your sister."

As the Jag rolled away, a red Jeep Wrangler loaded down with surfboards pulled into the vacant space next to me.

Dirk reached into the back seat, held up a pair of faded yellow swim trunks, and tossed them my direction. "You ready to catch some waves?"

"Now?"

"I only get an hour for lunch and I'm not going to spend it in a parking lot. You want to talk, we do it in the water. See you on the beach."

# CHAPTER THIRTEEN
# SURF'S UP

**I** stood at the tide line with cold water swirling over my bare feet. In addition to the swim trunks, Dirk had loaned me a full wet suit, but that did nothing to take the chill from my frozen toes. Dirk had on a surf vest and surf trunks. He did not seem bothered at all by the chilly water.

"We paddle out, clear those breakers, and wait for the set," he instructed.

"I only wanted to ask a few questions."

"So ask when you reach the lineup."

He splashed into the water and with a few quick strokes left me standing at the water's edge. Taking a few tentative steps forward, I lay down on the long board and began paddling. Every few seconds white water rolled over me, shoving me back. It took all my energy to keep the board moving forward.

When I finally reached the last line of breakers, he asked, "You the one who stole my canoe?"

"Yeah," I huffed. "Where you going now?"

"Outside. Set's coming."

I lifted my head and looked at the horizon. Nothing. Not even ripples from fish jumping. The sky had lightened to a pale blue. High clouds scudded overhead. I slapped the water and followed Dirk toward the imaginary "set."

"Is this a good break?"

Dirk glanced over his shoulder. "Not really. Hardly ever gets good except for hurricane swells. But if you're a surfer, whaddya gonna do?"

I couldn't imagine what kind of shape you had to be in to surf. In just the few minutes I'd been paddling, I could already feel my calves starting to cramp and my arms ... my arms felt like limp noodles. "You could surf somewhere else."

"Going to Costa Rica in a month. It'll be my second trip this year. But I grew up here. I can't imagine living anyplace else. What was it you wanted to ask me?"

I felt anxious to get to the bottom of what had happened to my sister. I would have preferred to question Dirk in the parking lot because splashing around on a surfboard was a huge waste of time: time Wendy did not have. For a few seconds I thought about going back in and catching the shuttle. I needed to check out Turtle Dove Estates, the place where Wendy's bike had been spotted that morning. Maybe there was a clue there that might point me to where she was being held.

But having gone to all the trouble to suit up and paddle out, I decided to press Dirk on his whereabouts during Wendy's abduction.

"Last night, right before the police arrived, where were you?"

"Why? You think I had something to do with what happened to your sister?"

"I saw you standing near the cart path. You must've been close to the boathouse to get there that quickly."

"I was."

Without elaboration, he paddled straight for the smooth green wall towering over us. He pivoted the board quickly and reversed course, took three forceful strokes, and jumped to his feet. With his lanky frame arched backward, he looked like the pictures you see in surf magazines of soul surfers. I managed to clamber over the wave just as it broke under me. There wasn't enough time to clear the second wave; I was too far inside, so I frantically kicked and clawed and spun the board around at the exact moment the wave began to rise beneath me. As the board slid forward, I grabbed the sides and pushed myself first onto one knee, then my feet.

The surfboard shot down the wave.

I bent my knees and felt the fins respond to the shift in weight and turn the surfboard. I cranked a bottom turn and brought the nose around, drifted up the face, and made a slight correction that, for a few moments, kept me tucked in the pocket. Then suddenly, the wave's smooth, green wall slammed into me and knocked me off, burying me beneath cold salt water.

A half hour later I sat on cool, dark sand with the sun warming my face. My feet felt numb, but I didn't mind. Surfing, even in small waves, was way better than snowboarding at a crowded ski resort.

"I was at a coffee shop near the marina." Dirk sat beside me with his wet suit tank top peeled to his waist. "That's where I was last night, hosting a Bible study at the coffee shop."

"How many in your group?"

"Last night? None. I'm a member of the International Christian Surfers Association. Our numbers fluctuate."

"You know, you're the second person I've met today who mentioned something about a Bible study."

"This is the Bible belt, bro. Get used to it."

I hesitated for a moment before saying, "So ... nobody can say for sure you were really there?"

He cocked his head and smirked. "I guess not. I help run the coffee shop sometimes, but like I said, on Wednesdays we use it for the Bible study. The staff leaves at eight since I'm there. Why? You really think I'd dress up like a zombie and take your sister?"

"Honestly, I don't know what to think. Obviously, you're in great shape. I mean, you could probably hold your breath for, what, a couple of minutes if you have to?"

"Longer. Three minutes easy if I'm not exerting myself." He jumped to his feet and peeled off his wet suit. "Lunch break is almost over, so I'd better get going."

*Three minutes. Just long enough to swim from shore, surface, and grab the canoe. What if Dirk saw me talking with Officer McDonald after the disappearance, became concerned, and warned the receptionist to keep an eye out for me? Maybe that's why Officer McDonald spent so much time answering my questions earlier today. It could be that Dirk told McDonald to learn all he could about what I knew, then debrief him in the conference room. The two men had looked as if they shared a secret. Had Officer McDonald hurried me along so the pair could discuss what to do with the nosy Nick Caden?*

We'd almost reached the parking lot when Dirk said to me, "Sorry 'bout your sis. Must be hard on you and your parents, but try not to worry. It's probably like Officer McDonald said: she spent the night with friends and now she's too scared to call because she knows when she does, your parents are going to be mad at her. Thing is, no matter how upset parents get, they love their kids and just want them back home safe."

"I appreciate your concern. I'll pass it along."

Resting his hand on my shoulder, Dirk said to me, "Also tell them I'm praying for your sister."

I studied those chlorine-blue eyes and sensed Dirk the surfer and Bible study leader would pray for Wendy — that he genuinely cared about her. Problem was, the really good liars are like that: smart, credible, and dangerous.

# CHAPTER FOURTEEN
# I'M A DEAD MAN

The shuttle let me out in front of the entrance to Turtle Dove Estates. I crossed the grassy playground and approached two mothers sitting on a bench. One was changing a diaper; the other rode a toddler on her knee. When I asked if either of them had heard about a missing bike being found, the young mom stopped bouncing her child and pointed to the end unit of a complex.

"I saw patrol cars there this morning when I was jogging. A couple of officers loaded it in the trunk and drove away."

I thanked the women and strolled to the front of the building. Without being too obvious, I gave the place a once-over.

Faded brown siding covered the exterior. On the roof there were signs of missing roof shingles. The hedge growing under the front window needed trimming and the porch railing, a fresh coat of paint. I shoved my hands into my pockets and continued to walk along the sidewalk. At the corner, I knelt as though tying my shoe. When I looked back, the two moms were pushing strollers in the opposite direction.

I fumbled with the knot in my sneaker, counted slowly to ten, and returned to the unit. Standing at the bottom of the steps, I found a place where the ends of red-tipped bushes had been snapped back. There was the slightest hint of tire tracks in the dirt next to the steps.

I took a deep breath and approached the front door, knocked, and waited.

*What if it's a setup? The caller warned that it was what he or she wanted. Did Officer McDonald feed me the information knowing this was exactly what I'd do?*

Mosquitoes sang into my ears. In the adjacent unit, a dog barked. I pressed my ear against the door. No voices or music or television set blaring. This place wouldn't be this deathly quiet if my sister were hanging around.

After my second knock I tried the knob. Locked. Taking a quick look up and down the street, I checked to see if anyone was watching. When I felt certain no one was, I snuck around back.

Rusty patio furniture sat on the cement slab. Weeds grew between cracks. A window screen lay against the side of the unit. I pressed my face to the sliding glass door and peered inside, looking past discolored floral-print drapes. There were white baseboards showing scuff marks, linoleum flooring starting to peel, fast food bags and soda cups piled on the round glass breakfast table. I tested the door. It rattled open on a wobbly track.

"Hello, anybody home?" I waited several seconds. "Wendy?" When no one answered, I stepped inside.

The place smelled musty and reeked of garbage. I inspected the fast food bags, two from Buffalo Bob's Burgers, the other McDonald's. I knew Bob's. Back in Wichita we'd eat there sometimes. Buffalo Bob's was a local company with stores throughout Kansas. Question was, how did bags from this particular burger joint end up in a townhome on Palmetto Island?

Inside the first bag I found two crumpled burger wrappers smeared with ketchup and an empty sleeve of fries. The date on the sales receipt matched the exact day we'd left Aunt Molly and Uncle Eric's cabin and began driving to Palmetto Island. The receipt in the second bag was from two days later. I couldn't remember our exact route, but I was pretty sure we'd taken I–35 south to Oklahoma and turned east toward Arkansas. Along the way I'd seen a couple of Buffalo Bob's signs outside Oklahoma City. I wondered, were I to check, if I'd find that the store number on the receipt was from the Oklahoma City area.

For a long while I clutched the two receipts in my hand, staring at the dates, pondering their possible meaning.

Possibility number one: Zombies are the *almost* dead. A person or persons knew about our temporary move to Uncle Eric's lake cabin and somehow learned about my father's scheduled interview with Ms. Bryant. Then said individual sent the unflattering letter of recommendation (knowing it would arouse Ms. Bryant's interest), tailed us to Palmetto Island, and waited for my parents to leave for their dinner meeting, then stalked Wendy and me to the boathouse and grabbed her. The person must've seen me pick the lock and steal the canoe. Or maybe not. Maybe swimming out to the boathouse was a last-second decision. But why dress up in the Heidi May Laveau outfit? Why not wait until we were back onshore? And why take Wendy (or me, for that matter)? I mean, there was no way I could give someone their life back unless … unless the individual needed my organs. *Is that what this is about, harvesting my organs for someone who is dying?* Immediately I rejected that idea. It was too farfetched.

Possibility number two: Monsters are real and a dangerous individual took my sister, the letter was sent by an accomplice from Kansas, and the food bags were shipped by the accomplice and planted in the townhome to throw me off. Leaving Wendy's bike outside the townhome would arouse suspicion and once Officer McDonald located the canoe and bike, the search for my sister would switch from Savage Island and the creek to combing the island. The email warned me to keep quiet. I hadn't shown Dad's letter of recommendation to Officer McDonald or mentioned the phone call. One fact about sociopaths: they like seclusion and secrets. That meant I was the only one who knew about the Kansas connection.

*Kansas ... isn't that what Kat keeps calling me?*

Possibility number three: Kat was the kidnapper. What if Kat was not some playful friend trying to help me find my sister, but a seriously disturbed young teen? She seemed to know my every move. Was she stalking me? Had she meant to surprise me at the boathouse the night before, but then found Wendy already in the canoe? Was Kat vicariously living the life of Heidi May Laveau by dressing up as the dead girl and kidnapping boys and girls—and if so, why?

Possibility number four: Random, unrelated events. Maybe ... Wendy escaped from the prankster dressed as Heidi May Laveau and paddled the canoe to shore ... One of the kids from last night's campfire borrowed my sister's bike and dumped it in the bushes ... The tenant in the townhome lived in the Kansas-Oklahoma area and was a fan of Buffalo Bob's ... Matt found out about Dad's job interview and faked the letter ... After beaching the canoe, Wendy walked back, arrived while I was at the church with Kat, and found the condo locked. She crashed someplace and returned this morning, only to find we'd already checked out.

What if Wendy was, in fact, looking for us? What if she thought we went home without her? *Sure, that makes the most sense, but how do you factor in the picture of Wendy in the email and her terrified voice on the phone?*

Too many possibilities—too few hard facts pointing to a solution.

The clock over the microwave read 2:53 p.m. Three hours until dusk. I shoved the receipts in my pocket.

In the living room I found a plaid, swaybacked sofa. On the opposite wall stood an entertainment center housing an old flat screen television. The bunk beds in the first bedroom had the crisp, made look of professional housekeeping. Pillows fluffed, stuffed animals arranged for decoration. No damp towels in the middle bathroom. A master suite occupied the back bedroom. One dresser drawer stood partway open. Covers turned back, a pillow on the floor. Wash towel on the floor next to the bathroom door. Hanging over the bed was a portrait of a sailing dory. I eased closer, stepping over a single gray sock. *No way to know for certain if it's the same painting from the email, but it could be. It most definitely could be.* I wondered if I could pull the picture up on my phone. On a hunch, I walked across the room and stood in the corner looking back toward the bed and painting. I raised my hands to my face and imagined I was taking a picture. *Yes, the kidnapper would have been standing right about . . .*

From the kitchen I heard the patio door slide open.

My heart stopped.

Heavy footsteps clomped across linoleum flooring.

I hurried back to the doorway and looked down the hallway. A man-size shadow passed across the wall. Quickly I glanced around the room. No door opening onto a deck or balcony and no chance at all of opening the window without rattling the blinds. A cabinet door opened. Water ran from a faucet. A glass clanked on the counter. *Sneaking into the townhome was stupid. I should have sat outside and waited until the owner came home.*

My only hope was to reach the front door. I heard my pulse pounding in my ears. With each step, the gulping of someone drinking grew louder. Sweat trickled down my ribs. I reached the living room and managed to cross the room without alerting the person in the kitchen. My hand found the doorknob. I turned and pulled. The dead bolt bumped against the frame. With my back to the kitchen, I twisted the lever until I heard the dead bolt make a hard clicking noise.

The sound of running water stopped.

If I'd been smart, I'd have shot out the door. And I might have made it, too. But I had to see, had to face my sister's kidnapper. With my hand still on the doorknob, I peeked over my shoulder.

Officer McDonald stood behind me with his weapon drawn.

Possibility number five: Officer McDonald is the kidnapper and … *I'm a dead man.*

## CHAPTER FIFTEEN
# BUSTED

**W**ho let you in?"

Officer McDonald waited calmly for my answer, his large brown hands holding the gun on me.

My mind raced feverishly, eyes shifting as I searched for a way to escape. "The back door, it was ... open."

He holstered his weapon but continued to watch me carefully. "Open or unlocked?"

I tried to swallow but my throat felt like it was coated with dust. I needed a plan, one that did not involve getting shot as an escaping intruder, but my options were limited.

"Unlocked," I admitted.

He glanced quickly down the hallway, then back at me. "Anybody else here with you?"

I needed to settle my breathing and relax. Otherwise I'd make a mistake. Maybe my last one.

"No one, it's just me. I came by to see if I could figure out how Wendy's bike ended up outside this unit." Frantically, I tried to change the subject. "There's a portrait of a sailing skiff in the main bedroom. It looks like that one I saw in that email I received."

"That old thing? There's probably hundreds — maybe thousands like it on this island. It came with the unit."

"You mean this is ... your place?"

His pale-green eyes locked onto mine. "Bought it a few months ago as a fixer-upper to be used as rental property. So far it's worked out pretty well. Except for when someone breaks in."

McDonald carefully positioned himself so that he could quickly grab me if I went for the door. I had a pretty good idea what he had in mind. Tie me up and wait for darkness before hauling me away to the hideout where he kept Wendy.

"But when I spoke with Ms. Bryant, she told me you couldn't afford a second home on the island."

The muscles in his neck bulged. "Ms. Bryant ... if I'd waited on her help, I might have never gotten this unit. Thank goodness her assistant hooked me up with a mortgage company that was willing to work with me."

"Assistant? You mean Matt?"

"He took care of all the financing. He also manages the rental calendar. He's had someone in here since day one."

*Okay, so maybe I've misjudged him. Perhaps McDonald doesn't know he's leasing his townhome to a monster.*

"Do you know who's staying here now?"

McDonald rested his hands on his bulky gear-laden hips. "I do not. That's private information. But if you're suggesting I'm harboring a criminal ..."

"You saw the bags on the table, right? From Buffalo Bob's? I know that fast-food joint. We have them back home. Know what I think? I think—"

"What you think or don't think makes no difference. Fact is, you're trespassing ... again."

"So are you going to arrest me?"

"Haven't decided. Depends on if the occupant finds anything missing. Meantime, let's you and me take a ride."

"Where were you? I've been trying to call you."

Mom stood in the cockpit of the trawler with fists on her hips. I couldn't tell if her cheeks were pink because she was upset at me or because she'd forgotten to put on sunscreen.

"I need to speak to you two about your son, ma'am."

I stood beside Officer McDonald on the dock. As soon as he'd spat the word "son," I dropped my head and focused my attention on the barnacles growing on the trawler's hull.

McDonald held his hat in his hands and kept running his thumb along the brim, waiting for Mom's response.

Dad poked his head out of the companionway hatch. "Is there a problem, officer?"

"Yes, sir, there is. I was just explaining to your wife that we need to have a chat about your son and what he's been up to."

Dad glanced over to me, a look of disappointment on his face. I felt like an ant; small, insignificant, and about to be stomped on.

"If it's about that canoe he stole, we'll pay for whatever damages there are," Dad offered.

"I'm afraid it's more serious than that. May I come aboard?"

Dad waved us onto the trawler. I chewed my lip, fighting the urge to explain what I'd found in the townhome and my theories for who was behind Wendy's kidnapping. Officer McDonald still had not told me if I was being charged with breaking and entering, but the fact that he had not taken me to his office was encouraging. I followed him aboard and noticed our luggage stacked beside the little door leading into the cabin.

"Your son broke into a townhome," Officer McDonald stated.

Mom gasped. "What?"

"Is he under arrest?" Dad asked.

"Why would you do that, Nick?"

"Why do you think, Mom? I was trying to find Wendy."

"Your son entered through the patio door. Thankfully, it was me who found him snooping around and not the person renting the unit."

"What were you thinking, son? You could've been shot." Turning to Officer McDonald, my father said, "Sometimes Nick gets so wrapped up in this TV Crime Watchers business that he forgets he's not a real detective."

"I don't understand," Mom cut in. "You've never broken into a house, not ever."

"Unless you count the boathouse," Officer McDonald countered.

I knew better than to open my mouth. Chewing on my lip, I propped my backside on the stern railing and stared at the pile of suitcases. For a split second I got excited, thinking that Wendy had escaped from the kidnapper, found her way to the marina, and we were leaving. But then I remembered that was impossible — my sister's kidnapper still had her and would keep her until I solved the riddle of who snatched Wendy.

"What your son did is bad enough, but there's another thing that concerns me," Officer McDonald was saying. "Earlier, when I mentioned that we'd found your daughter's bike, I told you we thought she was staying with friends. I still think that's the case. There are several girls your daughter's age staying in Turtle Dove Estates. What I didn't mention is that her bike was found outside my townhouse."

Dad's eyebrows shot up. "Yours? Are you saying Nick broke into your home?"

"Yes, sir. It's a rental property. I would have already notified the occupant, but the rental agency handles everything and I don't have the contact information. On the way here I called over to the rental office and let them know the situation in case the renter finds anything missing and wishes to file charges."

*Missing? My sister is what's missing. That's what you should be focused on.*

Mom scowled. "You have some serious explaining to do, young man."

"I swear, I didn't *do* anything seriously wrong, Mom. I was just trying to find out where Wendy is."

"Like you don't already know," my mother shot back.

I studied her face—and Dad's—wondering how much I should share. Maybe if they knew the truth, they wouldn't care that I'd slipped into Officer McDonald's townhome and almost discovered the identity of the kidnapper.

"Here's what I know," I felt tempted to blurt out. "I know Officer McDonald *probably* rented his place to someone living near us in Kansas and that someone *probably* wrote a bogus recommendation letter for Dad and mailed it to Ms. Bryant. Why, I *do not* know. That person might even be working with someone from Ms. Bryant's office, like Matthew Carter, because in the email, the kidnapper claimed credit for lining up your business dinner. The sales receipts from Buffalo Bob's can *probably* tell us who that someone is. I have them in my pocket. I also know the painting in Officer McDonald's master bedroom is *probably* the same as the one in the email I received. The other thing I know is that Wendy *probably did not* run off and spend the night with friends. *That* is what I *probably* know."

Of course, I didn't say any of this. How could I? The kidnapper had warned me to keep quiet or else. Instead, I nodded in the direction of our luggage stacked by the companionway door and asked, "Are we going home?"

"The charter company needs the trawler for another group that's coming in," Dad explained. "Something about a catamaran sailboat not being available."

"But we're not leaving the island, are we? At least until we find Wendy?" I couldn't bear the thought of driving off the island and over the bridge knowing Wendy was possibly locked up in some monster's basement and terrified that she'd never be found.

"No, of course we're not leaving, but believe you me, there'll be serious consequences for both of you when your sister does finally come back from wherever it is she's been."

"We'll find a motel," Dad offered. "Something cheap." He picked up Mom's bathroom bag and set it on the dock.

"We should have been gone hours ago," said Mom, piling on, "*but I couldn't reach you on your phone.* Of course, if we knew where your sister was, we wouldn't even need to get a room. We could pack and leave."

My parents didn't get it. Neither did Officer McDonald. They still thought Wendy's disappearance was my fault. *It's probably best that they think she's hanging out with friends,* I thought. *If Mom and Dad knew the real deal, they'd flip for sure.*

"So what's next, officer? Can Nick go with us or are you going to arrest him?"

The way Mom asked the question I almost got the impression she was hoping he would.

"Like I said, ma'am, it's up to the person renting my townhome. If the individual doesn't want to press charges, I'll let your son off with a warning."

"Great. Nick, grab your bag," Dad said "I left it in the front bunk of the trawler. You can load that dock cart and roll it up to the parking lot while I drive the car around. I'll pick up your mom and you there."

"What if Wendy shows up while we're checking into a motel? How's she going to know where to find us?" I didn't mention that this would be impossible, since Wendy knew nothing about their being at the trawler.

"Your son has a point," said Officer McDonald. "Someone should probably stick around. You know, in case your daughter comes looking for you."

I wasn't sure Officer McDonald meant for me to see him wink at Dad, but I did. I also noticed Dad give Mom a slight nod, as though he anticipated I might ask to hang back. Mom and Dad still did not believe Wendy's abduction was real; they had made that clear. I guess they figured as soon as the coast was clear I would contact my sister and tell her she could come out of hiding. Regardless, if I was going to find Wendy, I could not be cooped up in a motel room.

"Can I, Dad, please?"

"Sylvia, what do you think?"

"Why are you asking me? It's not like Nick is going to listen to us, anyway."

*Ouch!* I could tell by the tone of her voice she was upset—or was *trying* to sound upset. But I sensed she and Dad had expected me to ask if I could hang back. I think my parents believed as soon as they drove away I would contact Wendy and make it appear as though she'd escaped from her kidnapper.

Minutes later I stood in the parking lot, waving to my parents as they sped off in the Buick.

"Final time—are you positive you do not know where your sister is?"

I returned Officer McDonald's sympathetic gaze. I shook my head, "No, sir, I do not."

"In that case you'd better hope we find her and soon. It'll be dark before you know it."

As soon as Officer McDonald left, I hurried over to the fuel docks. Kat was pumping fuel into the tanks of a sport fishing boat.

When she saw me coming, she finished topping off the tank and straightened. "Hey, sorry you got booted off the *Ms. Fortune*."

"No worries. Mom looked pretty happy to be moving into a fleabag motel."

"How'd your visit go with Officer McDonald?"

"Not well." I explained how I'd quizzed him about my sister's disappearance and received the third degree from him in return. I told her about touring the fancy beach house with

Ms. Bryant, surfing with Dirk, and how I had been caught inside Officer McDonald's townhome. "I have a pretty good idea of who has my sister, but I'm going to need your help."

Kat laid the hose on the dock and threaded the cap, closing the fuel tank. "Oh? Doing what?"

"You said earlier you could run me out to Poke Salad Annie's place. Does that offer still stand?"

"Sure, why?"

"I need to bait a trap."

"Oh, what sort of trap?"

"One that catches zombies."

# CHAPTER SIXTEEN
# SWAMP WATER

**W**hile Kat went off to check with her Uncle Phil about borrowing a small runabout, I plopped down on a dock box and laid out the puzzle pieces of my sister's abduction.

Sneaking into Officer McDonald's townhouse had been a lucky break. Sure, it got me in hot water, but seeing the portrait of the sailing dory had confirmed my initial suspicions. Someone—maybe Officer McDonald or Matt, but probably the person renting the unit—had taken the picture of Wendy. I pulled Dad's letter of recommendation out of my back pocket and studied the signature: "K.G.B. Savior." *Savior of what? Is it some kind of code? A clue? The letters of a radio station?* I thought about how my editor would sometimes rearrange the letters of his name to create an alias for a story he'd written. The word "Calvin," for example, became "Anvil C." "Nick" could be turned into "C. Ink."

For a few moments I mentally moved around the letters of the name "K.G.B. Savior" but could not create anything close to a word or phrase that made sense.

"All set to go?"

I hurriedly put away Dad's recommendation letter. "What time is it?"

"Almost three thirty."

"Better get going. Last night it was pitch dark by seven."

High tide surged through the marsh, swelling over the creek's muddy banks. The sun had begun to bank toward the west, turning the water a copper-brown. What little breeze there was came from the south and brought with it the salty smell of the ocean.

I sat on a bench seat directly in front of the center console of the runabout, my bare feet resting on a white cooler. Kat assumed a position behind the center console, one hand on the shiny silver steering wheel, the other resting on the throttle lever. She'd turned a pink ball cap backward on her head. A small square of teal canvas that stretched above the console shaded her sun-browned face.

I squirted a glob of banana-scented sunscreen onto my palm, flipped back the shaggy ends of my hair, and lathered my neck and shoulders. My skin felt like I had a thousand tiny needles stabbing me from where the sun had burned my neck.

"Hey, Kansas, when you're done with the sunscreen, toss it back."

I passed the tube around the Plexiglas windshield. "Does the phrase 'K.G.B. Savior' mean anything to you?"

"Dudden to me, why?"

"Wasn't sure if it was a religious term or something."

"Well, the radio station in Savannah used to be WKGB but that got changed a while back. Now they go by the letters WSAV. How come you're asking?"

*KGB? SAV? Okay, so add another possible scenario to the list: Officer McDonald's cousin took Wendy, or maybe McDonald himself, and all this really is part of a radio station publicity stunt.* Of all the possibilities, that seemed the most likely.

And it gave me hope.

Hope that everything would work out. If it was a prank, as Officer McDonald had suggested at the very beginning, then when we did find Wendy she could be unharmed and maybe even a little excited (later) to know she was part of a radio promotion. I could see her texting her friends and telling them how she'd been kidnapped by a radio show personality as part of a zombie festival.

Without trying to sound too excited, I said to Kat, "I'm just trying to connect the dots; that's why I asked about the letters KGB."

Kat slowly spun the steering wheel and we made a lazy one-eighty turn.

I got up and joined her at the console. "Are we heading back?"

"If you'll look up yonder to your right, you'll see that green buoy is our next marker. After that, there's a red one on our left. And those birds over there? They're standing in about six inches of water."

I looked at where she pointed and spied the red cone-shaped float bobbing in the water. "How come they're shaped differently?"

"So when it's dark you can see which side of the channel you're fixing to run aground on. The reds are nuns, greens are cans."

"Speaking of nuns, earlier today you mentioned something about leading a zombie Bible study. Were you pulling my leg?"

"Ha-ha, good one, Kansas. And no, I was dead serious." She nudged me in the ribs. "See, I can tell a funny, too. You're free to join us this weekend. That is, if you're still around."

"The guy running the activities center, Dirk, he told me I'm in the Bible belt. What did he mean by that?"

Kat turned the boat to the left after we passed the green marker and we continued zigzagging our way toward the larger body of water.

"If you look at a map of the United States, there's a clump of states running from Virginia down to Florida and west to Texas. Those used to be the Confederacy. Uncle Phil says when he was coming along, most everyone in his town went to church — even those who did'n believe in God. He said if you wanted to get business done, that's where you were on Sunday mornings."

"So around here, churches are like country clubs."

"Did'n say that. I was only pointing out that's how it used to be. Our Bible study is different."

"Because it's for zombies."

"Right."

I gestured toward the next marker. "We're about to hit that red float."

"Buoy, it's called a buoy. Float is something you take to the pool. And I'm all the way over here because I know for a fact there's a shoal running out into the middle of the channel that's not marked. Once we clear that we'll be in the Savannah River and I can let her rip."

"My dad's aunt goes to church. She says Christians will rise from the grave someday. Said that's why she's not afraid of dying. What do you think?"

"I think you'd better hang on."

She slammed the throttle forward and the boat shot across the water like a rocket. Wind snapped my hair; spray soaked my face. I stood with my legs spread wide to keep from stumbling backward.

By far the tour of the beach house and surfing lesson from Dirk had been the best part of my trip. I knew Mom hated the idea of living on the coast, but I hoped Dad got the job with Ms.

Bryant. Deep down I knew my parents loved each other but the financial stress of the past few months had set them on edge. Moving to Palmetto Island would give all four of us a chance to start over. Assuming, of course, I found my sister alive and safe.

We raced up the river, the motorboat's loud outboard drowning out all conversation. After probably five minutes, Kat backed off the throttle and aimed us toward a marshy area. We went chugging into a wide creek. Soon the river sounds of boat traffic faded. A couple of minutes into the maze I was completely turned around without any clue as to how to get back to the marina. Kat didn't seem fazed in the least by the web of intersecting creeks. She worked the throttle and shift lever, easing past submerged logs and over the shallow bottom as if she'd done this hundreds of times, and I supposed she had. This was her backyard, after all. I got to thinking that if someone needed to dump a body where it would never be found, Kat would be the perfect person for the job.

Just when I thought we'd hit a dead end, Kat nosed the front of the boat into a patch of reeds and we coasted into a narrow canal. Razor-sharp fronds grew thick along the shore. A gazillion bugs vectored, forming a dense cloud around my head. Behind the boat, a plume of mud expanded from where the prop dug into the bottom. Kat shut off the outboard and lifted the prop clear of the muck.

She handed me a boat oar. Together we began poling our way up the canal, pushing ourselves off the creek's banks as we moved toward the low-scrub island looming ahead.

"Here's the thing about church," Kat said at last. "Folks can poke fun at Christians and that's fine. Can't say as I blame 'em. I hate phonies and hypocrites same as the next person. The ones that really get under my skin are those who *say* they're Christians but don't act it. Either get on the bus or get off, but don't make the name of Christ a bad word to people that don't know Him, you know what I mean?"

"Wow, I didn't mean to start—"

"I ain't done yet. Thing I can't stand most of all is folks calling me narrow-minded and stupid just because I happen to believe in the Bible. For crying out loud, there would not *be* an America if it weren't for people believing in the Bible."

"I never said you—"

"Let something really bad happen to somebody and first thing they say is, 'Oh my God.' And He is. He's your God. And my God. And the only God there is."

"I wasn't trying to pick a—"

"But things have gotten so messed up that folks will put up with most anybody except a person that believes in Jesus."

"You done?"

"Mostly, yeah."

"What I was going to say is, the past couple of months I've been reading a little bit of the Bible each day."

"You have?"

"Dad's Aunt Vivian gave me a copy. It was sort of like a family heirloom. I promised her it would do more than sit on my bookshelf. I'm still not sure I agree with all the rules and stuff, but some stories are pretty cool. I especially like the one where the bald guy sent a bear chasing after a bunch of punks who were calling him bad names."

"I've never read that."

"I forget where it was. In the old section, I think."

The canal widened and we began paddling under a shaded canopy of low trees knitted with Spanish moss. Long-neck egrets loitered on limbs and rotten stumps. Bugs zipped across the tea-colored water. Our boat's movement sent ripples advancing ahead of us. At last we came to a tilting pier partially buried among cattails and willow reeds. The boat bumped against a piling and we stopped.

"Up yonder is a path," said Kat. "Keep to it, and I mean right on it, and you'll do fine. Hundred or so yards in, and you'll find Poke Salad Annie's place." The pier looked unstable, the path, buggy. "If you get into trouble, you know what to do, right?"

"Pray?"

"I was going to say yell like a scalded dog, but praying ain't a bad idea either. Good luck, Kansas. I reckon you're going to need a ton of it."

## CHAPTER SEVENTEEN
# POKE SALAD ANNIE

**I** stood on the dock watching the boat back away. After a few minutes, my ride became lost in the maze of trees. I slapped at a mosquito on the back of my neck, heard the outboard fire, then turned and started walking up the dock. By the time I reached the footpath, the drone of the runabout was nothing more than a faint hum.

The sun's feeble light strained to pierce the canopy of limbs. I thought about the kidnapper's warning to me: *The dead come alive at dusk.*

A breeze rattled leaves beside the path, and mosquitoes feasted without mercy. The path was made up of crushed oyster shells strewn over squishy black mud. About twenty yards in, the route veered up and onto a dome of dark sand and hard-packed dirt. Judging from the increased elevation, the island appeared to be the remains of an old spoil area for inlet dredging, or perhaps an ancient burial site. I'd read in a magazine in the condo about how Seminole Indians ventured north from Florida to hunt panther.

The path ended atop the crest and at the edge of a clearing.

A weathered clapboard shack stood about twenty feet off the ground on knobby pilings. Its low-pitched roof channeled rainwater into PVC piping that emptied into a blue plastic barrel. Cords of cut wood stood stacked inside a lean-to shed. Beneath the shack was an assortment of tools: a shovel, a rake, a wooden wheelbarrow. Animal skins hung from ropes strung between the pilings. Skulls of various sizes lined the steps leading up to the porch railing. I wandered into the backyard and came upon a crude rotisserie built over a fire pit. Slabs of meat sizzled; juice dripped onto hot coals.

The smell of beef grilling reminded me of Dad's backyard barbeques, the ones we used to have when we had our own home and were (almost) one big happy family. Dad isn't a bad cook but he always ends up burning dinner, even when Mom warns (yells at him) to be careful. Some years ago Wendy began calling Dad's outdoor barbeques the "The Caden Sacrifice" and his contribution to global warming.

I was still thinking about all the good times we used to have before Dad lost his job when suddenly I heard movement behind me.

I whirled and found myself looking down the bamboo barrel of something like a blowgun.

The barefoot woman wore a flowery dress reaching to her knees, a necklace of bones, and a seriously wicked scowl. Her skin was the color of motor oil. Glossy black dreadlocks hung over yellow-brown eyes.

"What you be doin' sneaking 'round?"

"Kat," I stammered, "she ... dropped me off."

"Who dis Cat?"

"Works at the marina? She said she knew you." The old woman grunted but made no effort to lower the blowgun. "Told me you might know what happened to my sister."

"Hinny know all. Hinny heah tings odduh folks no kin."

"Hinny? Hinny who?"

"I Hinny!"

"Oh, Annie, got it. So do you know where my sister is and how I can find her?"

"Hinny don' know dat."

"But you just said you know all."

"All dat I know, I know. Dat I don' know, how can I know?"

"You know, what you just said makes no sense at all."

"Come. You tell Hinny 'bout dis bad, bad ting dat happen to you sistuh."

"You're not going to shoot me with that thing, are you?"

She cut her gaze toward the barrel of the blowgun. "Depends. You lie to Hinny?"

"No, ma'am."

"Ebbuh you do, I shoot you good." She eyed the end of the barrel. "Knock you out whit dis dart."

*No trouble from me*, I thought. *I don't want to become your next front porch rug.*

I followed her around the house. She walked barefoot on broken shells the way someone else might stroll down a beach. The inside of the shack was one large room with a kitchen in one corner and a sleeping area separated by bamboo bead curtains. Reptile hides and furry pelts were nailed to the walls: alligator and snake, fox and raccoon. The decor of mismatched furniture looked as if it had been purchased at a yard sale. The most interesting item in the room was an old-fashioned, foot-powered Singer sewing machine.

I pointed at the leathery skin draped across the sewing arm and asked, "What are you making?"

"Goat coat. Sit, Hinny fix you sump'n to eat."

"If it's voodoo gumbo, I'm not hungry."

"What dis voodoo gumbo? You nyam up! Now sit!"

I pulled a rickety chair from the wooden table and sat.

The old woman pulled a dingy drinking glass from the cabinet and turned on the faucet. Filling the glass, she slid it across the table toward me.

"How be Rina?"

"You mean Katrina?" I sipped. The water had the temperature of warm spit. "She's fine. She's coming back to pick me up. Thought I better mention that in case you're planning on making a rug out of me."

The old woman grinned. For someone living in a swamp, she had an impressive set of orthodontics.

"Stuff you, maybe. But rug?" She shook her head. "Too bony."

She opened the door to the cast iron stove and tossed a log in, sending sparks shooting onto the grooved-plank flooring. Without flinching, she stomped them out, snatched a wooden spoon from an overhead hook, and began stirring the black pot simmering on the stove.

The shack and surrounding yard reminded me of an article we'd featured on the *Cool Ghoul* website during our weeklong "Zombie Survival Marathon." The article had talked about the importance of protecting your home base from the undead.

*One critical element of zombie survival is the location of your fortress — the bunker where you will hide during the undead invasion. You want it to be in a remote location far away from people.*

A backwater bayou qualified.

*Elevated, if possible.*

Check.

*And fortified with an electric fence.*

I hadn't seen anything remotely like a fence, but maybe she didn't need one. Could have been that snakes and gators were her natural defense against marauding corpses.

*Dig traps fashioned with spikes and bait with meat to attract zombies.*

On my way up the path I'd spied several piles of strategically placed palmetto fronds, suggesting possible pits that might snag a zombie.

*Make sure you have a long-range weapon, as you will probably be shooting zombies from a distance.*

I didn't know if a blowgun qualified, but it was better than nothing.

"I know 'bout you mammy and farruh. 'Bout how day no get along."

"How could you? We've never met!"

"You tink you sistuh and you fix tings. Make one big happy fambly like was when you leely boy." She interrupted her stirring to wave the spoon at me. "Hinny hep you fix tings, but fus' you tell Hinny 'bout you sistuh."

So I told her.

I began with an explanation of how I wrote for the *Cool Ghoul Gazette* and that we'd received a comment from a reader on the *Cool Ghoul* website about the body of a girl who had died fifteen years earlier washing up on an oyster bed in Savage Creek. How before the authorities arrived, the corpse vanished, and I wondered if I came back at night at low tide if I might...

"What? See mo' dead peopo?" She angrily whacked the spoon against her thigh. "Dis bidness 'bout de dead, it no right."

With a grunt, she put the spoon in the pocket of her dress and went searching dusty bookshelves. After a few minutes, she paused, tapped a finger against the side of her head, and quickly hurried outside. Moments later she returned carrying a worn, leather-bound Bible.

"Hinny fuhget she go in da yard whit her Bible to pray fuh de spirit of dat mun."

"What man?"

She cut her eyes toward the open window that looked onto the yard. I walked over and stared down at the rotisserie.

"Don't tell me you're cooking a ... person."

"Shet yo mout! Hinny no like dat. Da mun, he no saved. Devil make 'im do plenty evil. Kilt dat goat, he did. Say he make curse from da blood and put a hex on a mun. But I pray. Ask God fuhgive dat mun."

She slid a chair beside me and opened the Bible, pointing to a page. "What dis say?"

I began reading aloud. "Whoever touches a human corpse will be unclean for seven days."

She flipped pages and pointed to another passage. "And dis one."

"Do not turn to mediums or seek out spiritists, for you will be defiled by them. I am the LORD your God." I looked up from my reading. "So?"

"You go to dat creek fuh to see dead peopo and what happen? You sistuh, she get tek, dat what. Curse on you, maybe. Only Hinny no b'lee in such tings. Know what Hinny tink?"

*No, please, tell me. I'm dying to hear.*

"Hinny tink some bad mun tek you sistuh. What you not tell Hinny?"

"Nothing, I told you everything."

She clamped her bony fingers around my wrist. "No lie to Hinny! Hinny know all."

"Except where my sister is."

"'Cept dat." She released my arm, got up, and went to the stove. Spooning the lumpy concoction into a wooden bowl, she set the porridge before me.

I bent forward and sniffed. "What's in it?"

"Hinny's secret recipe. Leb'n herbs and spices."

"Is one of those spices roadkill?" I watched her scowl deepen. "Kat said you use snakes and some other things."

"You try, taste fuh yo'self."

I dipped the spoon into the bowl and slurped. "Hey, this is pretty good. For voodoo gumbo, I mean."

"No gumbo, it soup! Corn crab chowder." She pulled her chair close and turned to another Bible passage. "Dis say God sent Elijah da great prophet fuh to see a widow who be running out of cornmeal and fatback. Elijah, he tell dis widow dat God provide for her. Only she no sure. God, he say he put back dat cornmeal an' plen'y fatback. Den dis widow, her boy get sick and die. Elijah lay on dat boy. Tree times, him did. Elijah, he pray fuh God to make dat boy live again." With her finger she pointed to an underlined verse. "And God, him dun dat."

"I'm pretty sure you can't bring back the dead by lying on top of them."

"Whit God you kin."

Quickly she flipped through the Bible, showing me other stories of dead people. In one passage, some people threw a dead man into a grave. When the body touched the bones of a prophet, the corpse sat up and crawled out. Another time Jesus stopped a funeral procession and ordered a dead son to rise from his casket. Later, that Jesus fellow told the dead daughter of a man named Jairus to get up and she did. Not long afterward, Jesus told a man who'd been dead four days to come out of a tomb.

I stared into those yellow-brown eyes and said, "So you really believe the dead can come back to life?"

"Bible no lie. Hinny see fuh herself!"

"You see dead people?"

"Whit faith eyes, yes."

"Okay, well, I don't have faith eyes."

"Someday maybe."

I slurped more chowder. The soup was excellent. And filling. Stifling a yawn; I asked, "You didn't poison me, did you? Or drug me?"

"What you be talking 'bout? It crab chowder like I say." Shaking her head emphatically, she added, "Hinny no do drugs. Bad tings, drugs. You no should do 'em, either."

"But you have that blowgun?"

"For gators and coons, no peopo."

I yawned. "Are you sure you didn't drug me?"

"What I just say? Hinny no like dat."

I searched the room for a place to sack out. "Regardless, I need to lie down. I feel a nap coming on."

She pointed across the room at a plaid sofa buried under pelts and hides. I followed her over and waited while she swept her work onto the floor. With a heavy sigh, I sank into mushy cushions, put my head back, and closed my eyes.

"Hinny hep you find you sistuh," she whispered, tucking a scratchy blanket under my chin. "Teach'a you how to see whit faith eyes."

I smiled. Moments later I heard a screen door creak open. Bare feet went padding onto the porch. I told myself I would rest for a few minutes. I told myself that Officer McDonald's cousin was behind the zombie stunt and Wendy was probably in a hotel suite in Savannah enjoying the good life at the radio station's expense — that my parents had probably been informed of the hoax by now and that Wendy would be waiting for me when I got back to the marina. Dad would land the job with Ms. Bryant, my parents would find a way to work out their problems, and we would move to Palmetto Island. That's what I told myself.

In other words, I lied.

I lay there, wondering if my plan would work. I couldn't imagine it would, but what choice did I have? Better to bait the trap and see than do nothing. The taste of the chowder lingered on my tongue. I decided the old woman was probably telling the truth. I'd been racing around all day trying to find Wendy without taking a moment to slow down, and now the soup, fatigue, and lingering effects of the sun warming me on the boat had finally caught up to me.

I listened for the old woman's footsteps and heard a chorus of crickets, the drip of the water faucet, and wind blowing through trees.

Then I heard nothing at all.

## CHAPTER EIGHTEEN
# DEAD TO THE WORLD

From the outermost edge of sleep, a rustling sound tugged me awake. I opened my eyes and stared at the ceiling. The moon's silver light bled through the window next to the sofa, illuminating knotted pine beams. Day had turned to dusk, leaving the room a purplish-black. No sign of the old woman. No sign of Kat, either. Just me, alone in a shack in the middle of a swamp.

For several seconds I remained on the sofa, listening, thinking about the kidnapper's chilling words: *The undead come alive at dusk.*

Dusk: the edge of night. Dusk: the darkest stage of twilight. Dusk: when monsters appear.

From somewhere beyond the end of the sofa came the sound of the swishing of fabric. I lifted my head.

Heidi May Laveau stood in the doorway. Her tattered dress dripped onto the floor, leaving a sodden halo around her blackened feet. Skin hung off exposed bone.

What do you do when you come face-to-face with the living dead? How do you react when your night dreams become an unholy nightmare? My heart slammed against the walls of my chest, and like a frightened child, I pulled the blanket fully over me until only my eyes peeped out. This was the thing I'd feared, the unspoken question that haunted me: *What if I'm wrong about the identity of the kidnapper? What if the dead don't stay dead?* The old woman had pointed to passages where the undead rose, walked and lived again, but for a lot of my friends and my parents especially, the Bible was nothing more than a collection of fables, myths, and superstitious stories. *What if they're wrong?*

Laveau moved with the halting rigidity of a mummy emerging from its tomb. With club hands, her outstretched arms banged against the doorframe like a monster finding its way in darkness. With an unsteady lurch, the dead thing pivoted and bumped the door open. In the moon's cool white light I saw the deep gash across her shoulder and the pale curve of bone protruding from gray flesh. *No way that's makeup; she even smells dead.*

The screen door slammed shut.

Dead feet clomped onto the porch.

I trembled among dark shadows, afraid of what would come next.

In a childlike voice I heard singing from the front porch.

*"Ring-a-round the rosie,*
*A pocket full of posies,*
*Ashes! Ashes!*
*We all fall down."*

I sat up and peeked out. Heidi May Laveau stood on the top step bathed in the moon's yellow rays. I had not expected her voice to sound so clear and fluty. Grunts and groans, those are the sounds of a zombie. In a clumsy wobble, the dead girl swiveled and bumped down the steps.

Slowly I peeled off the blanket.

I tested my legs. They worked. Given how severely my knees shook, I hadn't been sure they would. A quick survey of the shack confirmed that I was alone. I crept toward the door and peeped out. Laveau stood in the yard in all her gory grotesqueness.

*Okay, Caden, think this through—how do you want this to end? With you on that rickety dock searching for a way off this island or capturing the thing that has your sister?*

I took a deep breath and made my way onto the porch. As I started down the steps, I recalled a book I'd reviewed weeks earlier on the *Cool Ghoul Gazette* website. In it the author advised readers:

Sever the zombie's head. If that doesn't work, disassemble the corpse by hacking it into small parts. Finally, burn, bury, and pave over with top-grade asphalt. If you can plant your zombie in the middle of an interstate, so much the better. (Even if they survive, they will have a hard time dodging rush-hour traffic and thus remain occupied for hours.)

A few readers questioned whether this would actually work, but the book, *The Zen of Zombies: How to Get a Head and Keep It*, remained a top seller on our site, so I had to believe some of the information was accurate.

I reached the bottom of the steps and looked around at the assortment of tools scattered beneath the shack. I needed a weapon. Hacking up a zombie wouldn't be easy. I settled on an ax.

With each faltering step my heart beat faster. I kept telling myself it was all a prank, some elaborate stunt sponsored by the radio station, and that Wendy, my parents, and Officer McDonald were hiding in the woods ready to spring and shout, "Surprise!" But the farther away from the shack I walked, the faster my heart pounded, and the less sure I became that my plan would work.

*Trap a zombie—who am I kidding?* I mentally clicked off the crumbs I'd scattered for the suspects.

Crumb one: At the realty office I'd asked Matthew Carter if he knew about Poke Salad Annie. He did. Called her a swamp cracker. If he wanted to find me, he could and would.

Crumb two: While surfing with Dirk I mentioned that I might ride out to visit the old woman living in the swamp. He'd acted surprised, as if he'd never heard of such a thing, but if he was telling the truth about being from the Palmetto Island area, *how could he not know?*

Crumb three: While riding with Officer McDonald from his townhome back to the marina, I'd let it slip that I had one more person to question. When I'd told him it was Poke Salad Annie, he had warned me to be careful, that Gullah folk had peculiar ways and that occasionally "people go missing in that swamp." Was that a threat or genuine concern? Had he alerted his cousin from the radio station? I felt like in a few minutes I would find out for sure if Officer McDonald could be trusted.

Crumb four: Kat knew exactly where I was. In fact, it had been her idea all along to visit Poke Salad Annie. Now I had, and Kat (surprise!) had not returned after work as promised.

Crumb five: The old woman herself. She'd welcomed me into her home, fed me porridge, filled me with tales about dead people from the Bible, and promised to find Wendy. And perhaps she could and would ... at my expense.

I hung back, barely keeping the dead girl in sight for fear of getting too close.

I passed the fire pit with the rotisserie and, in the moon's glow, studied the carcass of grilled goat. I recalled the old woman's words: *Kilt dat goat, he did. Say he make cuss from da blood and put a hex on a mun.* What if Poke Salad Annie was the one killing goats, draining blood, and putting hexes on people? *And what if I'm the next victim of a curse?*

I stepped into the forest. A full moon played peekaboo above the treetops while somewhere to my left the unsettling chorus of frogs let me know the swamp's murky moat hemmed me in. Oily black roots grew along the ground in gnarled clots. Dark syrup oozed from silken cocoons hanging from limbs. The forest reeked of dead vegetation, stagnant water, and the sour odor of exposed mud banks. Coastal smells. The previous evening on my bike ride to the church, I'd inhaled similar odors and found them welcoming, but no more. Now the stench reminded me I was trapped.

The dead girl tromped deeper into the forest, her stiff frame tilted forward as she crashed through tendrils of vines knitted between twisted trees. With my surging pulse pounding in my ears, I kept my distance, staying just close enough to keep her in sight.

At last I came to a clearing. Ferns covered the ground, their green leaves shimmering with the dew of dusk.

About twenty paces ahead I saw the dead girl hesitate, as if unsure which way to go. I held my breath, half expecting her to whirl and charge at me. Instead she sniffed the air like a dog. I needed to breathe but didn't dare, not even a little. Suddenly she turned her head as if picking up a scent and pushed on, trampling ferns underfoot. At the far side of the clearing she plunged into a tangled fist of thorns and vine and melted into the woods.

With halting steps I entered the clearing. Ahead I heard crunching and snapping. I could almost taste salt as the night breeze blew in from the ocean. In the distance through a narrow slot in the trees, the moon's glow reflected off the water's oily sheen. *Maybe that's what she smelled,* I thought. *Dead low tide with its sour odor of rotting seaweed and stench of decaying crabs and fish.*

Another step, then another.

The noisy thrashing in the forest ceased.

I froze.

Only the scratching of wind in the trees drowned out the pounding in my chest. A cold finger probed my heart, pushing it upward until it caught in my throat. *Come on, Caden, you can do this, you have to.* One step, three, ten. My eyes darted side to side. I scanned the perimeter, certain she was watching me. Nervous sticky-damp sweat clung to my upper lip. My feet became clay, legs heavy logs. Then I heard ... moaning.

I whirled.

Nothing behind me. Just the rattle of dead leaves snatched by an autumn wind. I searched the forest, straining to see into the blackness. Once more there came a chilling groan. It seemed to envelop me as though a phantom creature hovered by my side. The hairs on my neck stiffened; tightness gripped my throat.

*There it is again!*

Slowly I lifted my eyes.

Poke Salad Annie dangled by her feet. Despite the vine

around her ankles, she'd managed to keep her knees together and her dress from fluttering over her head, and her long arms worked the gag over her mouth, trying to loosen it. It was tight!

She pointed, and I followed her wide-eyed gaze. She seemed to be studying something on the ground.

"Another trap?" I asked.

She moved her head in the affirmative.

I crouched. "Here?"

She blinked.

I swept the ax head across ferns in a slow helicopter motion. I'd made almost a full circle when suddenly a lasso coiled among the ferns snared the ax head. The handle leapt from my hand and went shooting skyward. The ax made a horrific crash as it smashed into a tree. Oscillating back and forth like a bungee jumper, the ax dangled overhead like some macabre executioner's weapon.

In disbelief I stared upward. "Great, perfect." I balled my fists on my hips and turned toward the old woman. "Anything else I should watch out for?"

"Mumm isfff caaah!"

"Say again, I didn't understand."

My sarcasm was a nervous reaction to the panic I felt bubbling inside me. Without the ax I had no way to defend myself. Worse, I now I had no idea where the zombie girl was. As soon as the words left my mouth, I felt bad. It wasn't the old woman's fault I lost the ax. I also felt bad I couldn't help her down, but she was, like, fifteen feet up in the air.

"Mumm aaurgh!" She was waving her arms now, gesturing at a break in the forest.

The shadowy tunnel of limbs hinted at a path. I examined the ground, inspecting every leafy fern. Taking small, careful steps, I approached the opening, peeled back thorny branches, and peered in.

There comes a point in any expedition when you know you should turn back. Admit you messed up and back away before you do something really, really dumb — like bump into a living, breathing zombie. I had reached that point hours earlier. If I'd been smart, I would have booted up my phone. Sure, it might have downloaded a virus from the Crime Watchers website. Then again, maybe not. I stepped onto the path. With a violent shriek, glossy black wings shot past my head. I labored to slow my breathing but could not. I was in full flight mode, ready to run screaming back to the shack.

I pressed on, leaving the old woman behind me.

About ten paces in, the path stopped. Palm fronds lay scattered over the ground. Slivers of moonlight broke through the treetops, illuminating something like a campsite or worship area. Conch shells lay arranged in a circular pattern, marking the outer edges of the place. In the center stood a cross, two benches, and a single palmetto tree.

Kat sat slumped forward with her chin resting on her chest and her back against the tree trunk.

Her hands lay in her lap, bound at the wrists with rope. There remained just enough of the moon's glow bleeding through the forest dome for me to make out the fist-size bruise on her right cheek. I couldn't tell if she was alive or not, but I feared the worst. She still wore her Palmetto Islands Marina ball cap, only now the bill hid her large opal eyes. A wide strip of tape sealed her mouth.

I wanted to run to her. I wanted to cut loose her bindings, hold her close, and tell her it would be okay. Kat had been my first and only real friend on Palmetto Island. She'd sought me out the night Wendy went missing and been the one who encouraged me to visit Poke Salad Annie. She was my cheerleader, always upbeat, nudging me in the ribs in a playful sort of way.

And now she'd come back for me and paid a heavy price.

Jogging past the benches, I hurried toward her. But I wish I hadn't. I wish I'd looked around first and checked things out. Part of it was out of guilt. She'd come back for me. But part of it was something else. A longing to be of importance to someone my own age in a way I never had been before. Love was too large a word. Love was the word of my parents, and look what had become of them. But I couldn't deny I was fond of her. I found her accent and folksy sayings funny.

I almost made it.

Another few steps and I would have.

But as I jogged past the wooden cross, I felt the palm fronds beneath my feet give way. For a split second I saw the earth yawn as if to swallow me. Then I slammed face first into cool, damp dirt. Air exploded from my lungs. My cheek cracked against something sharp and hard. I lay there for a few moments unable to move. I kept trying to make my lungs work. Breaths came in short gasps. When I could finally lift my head, I saw the grave was maybe four feet deep and covered with bones. I was about to attempt to crawl out, but heard someone approaching.

I jerked my head up. In the radiance of the harvest moon, Heidi May Laveau stood over me. A sickly smile spread across her face.

> "Ring-a-round the rosie,
> A pocket full of posies,
> Ashes! Ashes!
> We all fall down."

My plan had worked. Laveau had taken the bait. Only problem was, now I was trapped.

Quickly I looked around for a foothold. *If I move fast enough, maybe I can climb out and run back to the shack.* Before I sprang, the dead girl pivoted, put her hands up, and ... tumbled backward!

She fell into the grave as if in slow motion. Her head was turned, eyes looking down, as if trying to find a place to land. Her momentum carried her over and back and down. She hit her head. There was a loud snap. It was the sound of bone snapping or vertebrae shattering. Heidi May Laveau folded into a crumpled heap of decomposing flesh amongst a bed of bones.

For several long seconds I knelt there too stunned to move. Finally I summoned the courage to check and see if she was really, really dead. With trembling hands I brushed back the bangs of Heidi May Laveau. My thumb brushed across her forehead, found a seam along the hairline, and picked at its edge. Slowly I peeled her face back. I pulled rubbery skin over brow, nose, and chin until I found myself looking into the eyes of real estate sales assistant Matthew Carter. Carter expelled a chilling groan, then nothing more.

"Told you the undead come alive at dusk."

The booming voice called from above. I twisted and stared up at the dark figure standing over me.

"Don't get too comfy; I got a bed made special just for you."

The moon's shadow fell across the man's face, making it impossible to get a clear look.

I scampered away from the grotesque body lying next to me and cowered in a corner of the pit. "Who *are* you?"

"Your worst nightmare, Caden, your worst nightmare. Sweet dreams."

From out of nowhere a gun appeared in the man's hand. I felt a sharp electric pain in my chest and a sudden sinking sensation. The impact spun me, slamming me against the damp, earthen wall. My hands went to my chest. Through blurry eyes I studied the missile-shaped dart protruding from my shirt. My legs buckled. I crumpled into a heap, toppling forward on my face. Blackness descended like a veil and the idea passed through my mind that this was the last I would see of this life.

Before I could consider the weight of that terrible thought, a heaviness pressed me into the moist dirt and I was no more.

# CHAPTER NINETEEN
# ON MY DEATHBED

**N**ight.

A time of shuttered windows and bolted doors.

Night.

A time when monsters hide beneath your bed.

Night.

A time of death and darkness.

From somewhere beyond the groggy haze, the stench of burning meat pulled me awake. In my nightmare I had been trying to run from an alligator. The creature had escaped from the small pond behind our rented condo and shot toward my bike with the speed of a cheetah. Lizard claws tore away large chunks of grass while I tried to pedal away. In the dream I could not make my feet work. When I looked down I saw that my pant leg was caught in the chain, but by then the gator was upon me, its jaws opened wide, hook-shaped teeth dripping blood. The beast emitted a loud hissing sound, like a truck's air brakes, and chomped down, pulling on my leg until...

I blinked open my eyes. My face, arms, and neck were soaked from the heavy mist that pressed down upon me. The crescent moon sailed in and out of fog until lost behind a veil of grayness. Straining every muscle in my neck, I lifted my head and looked around.

I lay staked to a muddy creek bank with my ankles and wrists secured by ropes looped through four thick wooden stakes. Legs and arms stretched out spread-eagle style, feet slightly elevated on the short slope of shoreline. A campfire blazed brightly beyond the tips of my bare toes, its amber glow casting dancing shadows onto the misty marsh grass. Judging from the darkened stalks sprouting from the bog, the tide was low.

Dead low.

Back home in Kansas my father uses Daddy Ray's barbeque sauce when cooking ribs. Or did, when we had a home and a deck and gas grill. Daddy Ray's is a special blend that's packed in mason jars and sold out of the back of Mr. Raymond's pickup truck. No label on the jars. No FDA approval, either. A quart goes for ten dollars but it's worth twice that. Except when Dad burns the ribs to a crisp. Then, not even Daddy Ray's barbeque sauce can make the meat edible.

The carcass roasting over the spit appeared very, very well done—as did the rest of Heidi May Laveau.

The charred husk had been burned beyond recognition. No way to know if the thing on the skewer was animal or human, but I feared the worst. I feared the scorched dress smoldering on campfire embers was all that remained of Matthew Carter. Not that it mattered. I had a new monster to battle. One exceedingly more dangerous than a make-believe zombie.

"Had an uncle one time who bought a cadaver from a medical school." I turned my eyes away from the sickening sight and toward the sound of the man's voice. "He had it shipped to his farm outside of Denver. This was back in the sixties. Back then you could do that sort of thing without people asking lots of questions."

The man sat at the edge of my peripheral vision. He sat on a driftwood log with his back to me. He sat watching the creek the way a fisherman does when he's waiting for a fish to bite. I thought about what Kat said regarding Officer McDonald and her uncle. *Sometimes he and Uncle Phil will wet a hook together . . .* For several terrifying seconds I wondered if I'd guessed wrong about the identity of Wendy's kidnapper.

"Cadaver showed up in a wooden crate. Deliveryman dropped it off on my uncle's front porch. I would have loved to see the look on that driver's face when he unloaded *that* package."

The talking man had broad shoulders and a bull's neck. An ax rested against his thigh. *The old woman's ax, maybe. The one snatched from my hand.*

"Now my uncle had in mind to get him a skeleton. You know, like you used to see in old doctor's offices. The ones where the bones are all hooked together with wire. So what he did was, he took that cadaver and put it into a metal barrel and tried to boil the meat off. You have any idea how long you have to cook a thing like that?"

The man's cowboy twang set my heart to pounding. I knew that voice, recognized the silhouette of that muscled man. He haunted me in my dreams. And now I knew beyond a doubt I'd been right about the identity of Wendy's kidnapper. Problem was, I figured it out a half step too late.

"Three days that body stewed. Fourth day, my uncle got the idea he'd bury the body out back in his yard and let worms and bugs take care of things. That's how you get an elk rack, you know. Take the head and plant it deep. Come back in six months and you got yourself a clean rack. Add a little bleach and it's good enough to mount."

Cold water tickled my fingers. I jerked my head around and stared in horror at the surging tide. The tide had turned. Ripples sloshed up the muddy bank. The knuckles on my outstretched right hand appeared as small islands on a black sea.

"Uncle went to Wyoming on a hunting trip. Stayed gone two weeks. When he got home he found his prized cadaver missing. You know why they bury a body six feet under?"

All my attention remained directed at the expanding creek and my sunken hand. The rope cinched around my wrist became a gray dam holding back the flood. Then it, too, vanished.

"Hey!" The ax head jolted my ankle and sent a sharp pain up my leg. "I asked you a question."

In a tired voice I replied, "Because if you bury a body six feet down, animals can't smell the corpse rotting."

I forced myself to turn away from the encroaching tide. Given the speed of the current and gradual incline of the bank, I figured I had five minutes tops before I was underwater. Instead of panic, a strange calmness settled over me. Or maybe it was the beginning stages of shock.

I fixed my stare at the hulking shape. "Where's my sister?"

I needed answers. Not that answers would save me. I had no doubt that unless something changed, and fast, the muddy creek bank would become my deathbed.

The man stood and stretched. "She's around."

"You said you would swap me for her."

The man strolled over. Squatting on his heels, he peered down at me. "Ever seen how a gator kills its victim? What they do is, they take a body under and shove it under a log. Sort of like a dog burying a bone." He gave one of the ropes a tug, testing the firmness of the stake. "When they're good and hungry they come back. I'm thinking you'll make a bite-size snack, Caden."

Trying to sound more confident than I felt, I replied, "You can't murder people and get away with it."

Patrick Gabrovski leaned close to my ear and whispered, "Have so far, Caden. Have so far."

"No, you killed Bill Bell and got caught. I made sure of it."

"That was Pat Garrett, Wild West gunslinger and renegade actor. Besides, haven't you heard? I'm dead. Drove my truck into a bridge abutment this side of Loveland Pass. They had to identify my remains from dental records. Nasty business, burning a body. Stinks something awful." Gabrovski cut his eyes toward the blackened carcass. " 'Course, I'm pretty good at grilling. Hard part was inserting fake dentures into the gums of that hiker. Did you like the way I signed that fake letter of recommendation 'K.G.B. Savior'?"

"Was that a clue?"

"Killed … Gabrovski … Burned. Figured I'd toss you a bone. Shame you didn't figure it out."

"How do you know I didn't?"

"If you had, you wouldn't be sprawled out on this mud bank like you are."

I tried to swallow, but given the angle of my head, the saliva caught in my throat and I emitted a hacking, gagging sound.

"Better get used to it, Caden. In a few minutes that choking sound is the only noise you'll make."

I told myself to stay calm, not to worry. That as long as I kept him talking I had a chance. But deep down I knew I was a dead man.

Pushing down the panic I felt, I said, "Neat trick, getting Matthew Carter to dress up like a zombie. How'd you talk him into doing that?"

"Ego. Carter had his heart set on becoming an actor. I

convinced him I was filming another *Blair Witch Project* and wanted to cast him as the star."

"And he believed you?"

"I still have a few connections in LA. Not as many as I did, thanks to you and what happened in Deadwood Canyon. But I found an out-of-work studio producer to fake a casting call in Wilmington, North Carolina. Your boy Carter drove up. He had no idea he was the only person auditioning for the role. He came back here, I met with him at McDonald's townhome and explained how the first scene would go. He thought your sister was great, by the way. Kept telling me she was a natural."

He stood and returned to the campfire. "Bad thing about Carter was his attitude." Using the ax head he poked the carcass. A chunk of meat fell onto the embers and sizzled. "The boy had a hard time following orders."

I tried to shake off the mental image of Carter hacked to pieces and shoved onto the skewer but I couldn't. Fog trapped the stench of burned meat until that was all I could smell. "Why the zombie outfit? Seems like involving Carter was a huge risk."

"I needed to make you look foolish. It worked, too. Your parents—what's their opinion of you right now?"

"That I'm a liar and can't be trusted."

"There you go, same as what people think of me."

"But you killed someone." He whirled and with one hand swung the ax over his head. My heart stopped. The blade shimmered in the campfire's light. Then, like a lumberjack, he gently rested the long stock of the handle on his shoulder.

"If I'm dead," I said almost in a half whisper, "what difference does it make what people think of me?"

"Legacy, Caden, legacy. Character is the only thing we leave behind. How a man lived is what folks think of him. You stole my reputation from me when you pinned Bill Bell's death on me."

"No, Gabrovski, you did that when you pulled the trigger."

"Thing is, I can repair my reputation. And I will, just as soon as I'm finished with you."

"How?"

He stood over me, a wicked grin spreading across his face.

It hit me: our Crime Watchers website. "Oh, I get it. You think by gaining access to the FBI database you can alter the evidence against you. Or maybe create a new identity."

"I'm going to miss having you around, Caden, I really am."

Ripples lapped at my earlobes. I tested the stakes but there was no play at all, none.

"My parents are looking for me. I'm sure Kat told them where I am."

"Oh, I wouldn't put much stock in getting help from your mom and dad. They're ... tied up at the moment."

Salt water kissed my lips. The tide surged past my elbow, washing up to my armpit and sending my pulse pounding in my ears. Suddenly I wasn't so sure of my plan. Baiting Wendy's kidnapper had been a huge mistake, I saw that now.

With a wave of panic sweeping over me, I blurted out, "Let's make a deal. You take me and I'll help you create a new identity. One so good no one will ever know you were involved in Bill Bell's murder. Just let Wendy and Kat and the rest go."

"Like I told you on the phone, Caden. You're in no position to bargain."

I lifted my head to keep water from seeping into the corners of my mouth, but the creek became like a large blanket being pulled over me.

"Please, I'm begging you ..." Gritting my teeth, I breathed in through my nose.

Gabrovski placed his hand on my forehead. "Don't fight it. It'll be over soon." With his eyes locked on mine, he pressed my head down, pushing me under the water until mud oozed around my ears.

Salt water flooded my nasal passages and stung the back of my throat. For several terrifying seconds I remained rigid. Small bubbles escaped from my nose. Then I began to choke and buck. *Oh God, oh God, oh God ...* I arched my back and dug in my heels, and tried with all my strength to pull the stakes free. Gabrovski's hand pressed down harder, pinning me to the bottom. With an uncontrollable rage I flung my head side to side, all the while clenching my teeth together so tightly that my jaw throbbed.

With eyes open wide I stared through blurred blackness at Gabrovski. Stared until salt water stung my eyes. Stared until Gabrovski became an evil monster standing over my deathbed.

Slowly I closed my eyes and welcomed the end.

# CHAPTER TWENTY
# DEAD BUT NOT QUITE GONE

**November 1**
**Palmetto Island, Savannah, Georgia**
**10:57 p.m.**

Dear reader: If you reached this part of the Heidi May Laveau story, then you know I drowned. It couldn't be helped. Oh, I suppose if I had planned better and thought things through, I could have saved myself. But really, what fifteen-year-old has the skills and smarts to overpower a sociopathic killer?

And that's what Patrick Gabrovski is—a cold-blooded assassin with an inability to recognize others as worthy of compassion. You know, sort of like a zombie, only worse. Monsters like Gabrovski are fearless thrill seekers, incapable of having meaningful relationships. For someone like Patrick, a tormented soul who has suffered a lifetime of apparent injustices and rejection, murder seems like a logical solution to a perceived problem.

So he killed me.

Patrick, if you are reading this on the *Cool Ghoul Gazette* website, I congratulate you. You got away with it. You silenced the only person who knows your dark secret. The only investigative journalist who knows you died and remain alive.

The key—the one clue that helped me solve the riddle of who had my sister—came when I read that episode of *Grave Discoveries*. Took me a while to process the synopsis, but I remembered that the mobster in the show had been pronounced dead in the morgue. That removed him as a suspect and gave him the freedom to travel in disguise while executing his rivals. When I over-laid my father's letter of recommendation, the receipts from Buffalo Bob's, and heard Officer McDonald say that you died in a truck crash, I began to wonder if you might have seen that episode, too. I remembered you mentioned in Deadwood Canyon how you had always been infatuated with the Mafia's ties to Vegas. When you demanded on the phone that I give you access to the Crime Watchers website it all clicked. Only you would have known about our connection to the FBI's database and how it gives us the ability to monitor those in the witness protection program ... and keep tabs on those individuals who might want to harm someone in the wit-ness protection program.

So thanks, Patrick. Without realizing it, you solved the case for me. All I needed was a way to bait and trap you. The baiting proved easy. Catching you in the act, not so much.

And so here we are, you and me, dead but walking and working among the living.

I may not know where you are, but I know enough. And I will hunt you for as long as I'm dead.

Nick Caden: Dead but Not Quite Gone.

# CHAPTER TWENTY-ONE
# UP FROM THE GRAVE
# HE AROSE

Forty-nine minutes earlier ...

Twenty-two minutes and twenty-two seconds. That's how long Tom Sietas held his breath. In doing so he set a new world record. I would only need to hold my breath for two minutes. Three tops. I hoped by then Gabrovski would move on to other concerns, like disposing of Kat and Poke Salad Annie and the rest of the evidence that tied him to my sister's abduction.

The thing about holding your breath is that you need to conserve energy. The cocoon of cold creek water had the opposite effect. I felt my hands and feet growing numb. *Don't think about the cold, Caden. Focus on happy thoughts. Two minutes, come on, you can do this.*

I clenched my eyes shut and pictured an island. On the island stood a small bamboo hut. Strung between two palm trees was a hammock. I lay in the hammock. A sea breeze rocked me gently while surf boomed on an outer reef.

Small bubbles escaped from my nose. My back, shoulders, and head settled into soft mud.

*Forty-eight, forty-nine, fifty...*

On my imaginary beach I spied a figure walking toward me. A girl. She wore a ball cap and a faded denim shirt. In her hand she carried a pair of flip-flops. White shorts hugged bronzed thighs.

*Fifty-one, fifty-two, fifty-three...*

The girl from the beach ambled over and stared down at me. I pretended to be napping but through slitted eyes I watched her thump me on the chest. When I did not respond, she tapped harder as though trying to wake me.

My counting stopped, the imaginary scene vanished. I focused all my effort on keeping my lips sealed and tiny bubbles from escaping from my nose. I could sense Gabrovski standing next to me, his feet stirring the mud, legs shifting the flow of the current swooshing past.

He stood watching me for what seemed like hours. He had to be certain I really was dead.

I could feel panic clawing at the edges of my consciousness. The sensation of terror that seized my brain became so complete I had the feeling that any second my body would become unbolted from my brain, like a headless snake, and begin thrashing uncontrollably. *Leave, Gabrovski, just go!*

To take my mind off the presence of the monster standing beside me, I began counting backward from twenty. I reached the number nine before I sensed him sloshing away. I held out as long as I could and, with as much control as I could manage, allowed my head to float up. My mouth barely breached the surface, that's how fast the tide had risen. Parting my lips, I sucked air as quietly as a drowning person could. With lungs full, I settled, once more, on the bottom.

I chanced a full minute before surfacing again. I needed Gabrovski to think I was dead. That was the only way I would survive. But I almost waited too long. My lips barely broke the water on my second ascent.

With another mouthful of air, I sank. I began with my right hand, the stake under water the longest. Tug, pause, tug, pause, tug ... *Slow down, he'll see you ... Shut up, I'm out of air ... Mess up now and you die ... I'm dead anyway if I can't ...* The stake wiggled. Not much, but enough that I felt encouraged. I couldn't wait. I lifted my head. There was enough slack in the rope to allow me to slurp air. Back I sank and returned to the hard work of loosening death's grip upon me.

When it felt like my lungs would burst, the stake slipped from the mud. I breathed in more air and went to work on the left hand.

When at last my hands were free, I surfaced. With periscope eyes I took in the scene around the campfire. Gabrovski had peeled off his shirt. He was using it as a mitt to lift one end of the skewer. Walking to the edge of the creek, he flung the skewer, carcass and all, into the water. I watched him shoulder himself back into the shirt and begin kicking sand onto the embers. Nothing remained but fading smoke mingling with heavy fog. Satisfied, he pivoted and looked straight at me.

I froze. Had the fire still blazed, he would have seen me for certain. I couldn't be sure if my eyes, brow, and nose blended in with the dark water, but I hoped so. I thought he might wade out and check on me a final time, but the water's depth must have dissuaded him.

Finally Gabrovski went striding into the mist.

For several seconds I sat there, shivering. Chill and fright had left me exhausted. Finally I bent forward, found the rope securing my right ankle, gripped the stake with both hands, and pulled.

From somewhere in blackness I heard an almost imperceptible splash. I jerked my head and searched the creek. My eyes had begun to adjust to the dark. I scanned the water, taking in the horizon of deeper black and hedge of marsh grass on the opposite bank. The V-shaped wake of the beast gliding toward me came into focus. Instantly I understood why Gabrovski had tossed the carcass into the creek.

He had been chumming the water.

I almost got the first leg stake free before the gator attacked.

# CHAPTER TWENTY-TWO
# DEATH IS THE PITS

**A**lligators first appeared almost thirty-seven million years ago. Think about that. Gators have survived with relatively little innovation longer than pop quizzes have been around. New or old, it didn't matter. Seeing the gator's wake expanding toward me quickened my pulse and spurred me into action.

By some herculean effort I managed to rip out the stakes and bolt from the water. I'm pretty sure in one of my other stories I mentioned how I was a pretty fast runner. Not fast enough to outrun an adult alligator, but speedy enough. Gabrovski was a good five minutes ahead of me and I had a ten-yard head start on the gator.

I sprinted across the narrow spur of matted marsh grass until I was sure I'd lost the gator. Farther away from the creek the fog thinned, allowing for a clearer view of my surroundings. I stumbled upon a path of packed shells and followed it until the shack came into view. It sat in the shadows of trees, its tin roof melting into the mist. No lights on. I leaned against a tree and listened. Nothing. My only hope was that Gabrovski had arrived by boat.

Staying in the shadows, I walked down the path to the dock. A flat-bottom skiff lay tied next to the pilings. I jumped into the boat and felt the small outboard engine. It was cool. Gabrovski or Matthew Carter or someone else had been there a good long while. Lifting the cover, I removed the spark plug wire. It wouldn't stop Gabrovski but it might slow him down.

I retraced my steps up the pathway and continued around to the back of the shack. As I crept past the fire pit, I saw evidence from where Gabrovski had removed parts of the rotisserie. In the forest I skulked, eyes and ears alert. At last I came to where I'd last seen the old woman dangling upside down. Poke Salad Annie was gone. Only the eerie chill of cool evening mist cloaked the branches overhead. I glanced around, fear now replacing fatigue.

Then it started, a whispering exhalation blowing through the trees. *Huff, sigh. Huff, sigh. Huff, sigh.* My heart took a sharp upward lurch in my chest. The sound reminded me of a large winded animal, roaming the forest for prey.

I stood perfectly still, listening. The crescent moon sailed in and out of clouds, first illuminating the clearing, next leaving it in darkness. I couldn't be sure, but the breathing noise seemed to be coming from the zombie pit. Knees shaking, I carefully picked my way across the clearing and peeled back the briars in the thicket hedge.

The breathing sound seemed somehow familiar. I hunched my shoulders and stepped forward. Thorns picked at my shirt and scratched my arms, neck, and legs. I let go of the branches; they snapped back into place, sealing me inside the prickly cocoon. My panting now nearly matched that of the invisible beast that lay ahead. *Huff, sigh. Huff, sigh.* I moved ahead blindly, using my hands to probe the sides in order to remain on the skinny path, though "path" is hardly an accurate description. Finally I came to the end of the thicket. The monstrous breathing ceased. I pressed my hands against sharp barbs and pushed outward.

At that moment the moon sailed out from behind clouds and shone upon the scene. My eyes widened. Gabrovski stood beside the pit. Behind him a pile of dirt. I hadn't noticed the pile before. Probably because I'd been too busy trying to reach Kat. When I'd spied the pit before I thought it was part of the old woman's zombie compound, her way of keeping safe. But now I realized the hole was not a zombie trap at all, but a grave.

Kat's grave.

And I was too late.

The base of the palmetto tree stood empty. The gag Kat

had worn lay at Gabrovski's feet. I felt panic, anger, and fear all at once.

The loud breathing sound began again. *Huff, sigh. Huff, sigh. Huff, sigh.* The shovel's snuffing sound caused tears to well up in my eyes. My hands shook. *Run*, I told myself. *Run and kill that monster!* But I did not run. Instead I froze, unable to will my feet to move.

Gabrovski had removed his shirt. His shoulders glistened with sweat and dew. Spearing the pile, he worked tirelessly, tossing dirt into the trench. Burying Kat.

*Oh God, this can't be happening! Make it stop! Make him stop!*

I expected him to finish filling the grave, but instead he put away his shovel and went striding into the woods. I studied the shovel. All I had to do was sprint over, grab it, and wait for his return, hit him on the head, and …

Gabrovski came back before I could act.

And he brought company.

My sister walked in front of him. Gabrovski had one large, meaty arm around Wendy's waist. She was blindfolded and barefoot and he held her close to his sweaty chest. The sight of her stumbling along in that way sickened me. The two of them reached the pit. Gabrovski shoved Wendy to the ground and my sister screamed. A weak, wheezing, laryngitis-strained gasp. Gabrovski jerked her head back.

"Another sound," I heard him bark, "and I'll hurt you bad, understand?"

Sobbing beneath the blindfold, my sister nodded.

I had to do something, but what? Praying seemed like a waste of time. I wasn't even sure I believed in prayer. But then I recalled something Kat had said to me. *Let something really bad happen to somebody and first thing they say is, "Oh my God." And He is. He's your God.*

Gabrovski snatched up the shovel. With the cold detachment of an assassin, he returned to burying Kat. I hid in the thicket like a coward, frozen with fear. I couldn't imagine what Wendy was thinking. I'm sure she was terrified. The only reason I could see for Gabrovski to bring her to the grave was so she could watch before he ...

I shuddered at the thought. Instantly another idea came to mind and I recalled the words of the old woman. *Hinny hep you find you sistuh. Teach'a you how to see whit faith eyes.*

And she had. Wendy was there before me, alive ... for now. I shut my eyes and silently whispered, "God, help her, help me. Don't let my sister die, please, I'm begging You ..."

"Wendy?"

I jerked my head around. The voice came from behind me, from back at the clearing with the old woman.

"Honey, you out here? It's Dad. Where are you, sweetie?"

"This way!" I was tearing through the thicket, racing toward the sound of Dad's voice. "She's over here. Quick, hurry!"

Officer McDonald nearly knocked me down as he bull-rushed past me. I managed to get partway turned around just as he burst into the moonlight. There was a loud *pop-pop*. I couldn't tell who shot first, McDonald or Gabrovski, but then it became clear. McDonald whirled, and in a twisting fall, he landed on one knee and looked up at me. The front of his shirt had a spreading dark spot. Dropping onto both knees, he grunted and fell facedown.

Silence filled the void as the echo of gunfire died.

I stood trembling, horrified at the sight of Officer McDonald.

Dad came racing past me. "Wendy? Wendy!"

I pulled my gaze away from Officer McDonald and ran after Dad. He dropped to the ground and ripped the blindfold from Wendy's eyes. Pulling her into his arms, Dad rocked back and forth, wailing with such a deep, mournful cry that I felt my heart breaking. As soon as I saw Wendy was okay, I jumped into the pit.

Pawing at the dirt, I found Kat's wrist and began trying to dig her from the grave.

# CHAPTER TWENTY-THREE
# SAVANNAH DAYDREAMING

**Y**ou done?"

I ignored my sister's question. When you are writing your own obituary, it helps to ignore all distractions. Focus, that's the key. Focus and purpose. I had both.

I ran a quick spell check. No obvious mistakes or typos, but that didn't mean much. As I mentioned earlier, I'm a lousy grammarian. But I wasn't too concerned about proofing. I knew my editor would review the copy before it was published on the *Cool Ghoul* website. With a few keystrokes I inserted the date and time and reviewed the first paragraph of my article.

**November 1**
**Palmetto Island, Savannah, Georgia**
**10:57 p.m.**

Dear reader: If you reached this part of the Heidi May
Laveau story, then you know I drowned. It couldn't
be helped. Oh, I suppose if I had planned better and
thought things through, I could have saved myself. But
really, what fifteen-year-old has the skills and smarts to
overpower a sociopathic killer?

When I finished reviewing the article, I emailed the file
to Calvin. Minutes earlier he had informed me that the *Cool
Ghoul Gazette* website was back up. "No worries, bro. You did
good. I'm reading the breaking news coming out of Savannah
and it sounds like you nailed the zombie story!"

I allowed my gaze to linger on Calvin's words. My final
assignment and I'd hit a home run. Just like I'd dreamed. And
if things with Gabrovski had not gone so terribly wrong, I
could have continued investigating strange supernatural events.
Why, in just the past few minutes I'd come across a report of a
werewolf sighting in Maine. Bogus, obviously. There is no such
thing as a wolf man. But still ...

I sighed and tucked my tablet into my backpack. The night
had turned cool and clear, the heavy fog vanquished by a stiff
northwest wind. There was an amber glow to the west over
the Savannah skyline. Over my shoulder dock lights cast long
shadows across the stern of the *Ms. Fortune*.

"*Now* are you done?"

I turned my face toward Wendy and tried to smile. "I'm never done, you know that. And especially not when there are monsters like Gabrovski still at large. As long as he's out there, I'll keep looking over my shoulder, wondering."

"Okay, well, whatever. I'm walking up. Mom and Dad want to get going. Me too. I can't wait to get out of these stinking clothes and take a long, hot shower. I don't think I'll ever get my hair clean again."

"Sorry I got you into all this, sis."

"No biggie. I kept asking you to show me what you do and now I know. I promise I will never ever ask you to take me on another *Cool Ghoul Gazette* stakeout. Cross my heart and hope to—"

"Tell Mom and Dad I'll be right up."

Wendy threw her leg over the side railing and stepped onto the dock. Turning toward me she said in her raspy, laryngitis voice, "You know what? For a know-it-all, smart-aleck big brother, you're not so bad, Nick. See you at the van."

I watched Wendy trot up the dock toward the parking lot. The trawler's gentle rocking and the sound of small waves slapping the hull put me in a reflective mood. Leaning back in the captain's chair, I rested my bare feet on the steering console and enjoyed a few moments of Savannah daydreaming.

I had hoped Ms. Bryant would offer Dad the sales job. During the few minutes we'd talked, she'd seemed genuinely interested in Dad and his background. And when I'd mentioned how badly he needed work, she'd teared up a little. So from my way of thinking, we had already moved to Palmetto Island.

But when Gabrovski put two bullets into Officer McDonald and escaped into the swamp, all our plans changed. As long as Gabrovski remained at large, my family would be refugees in the FBI witness protection program. Gabrovski knew too much about us. And I knew too much about him. I linked my fingers behind my head and looked up at the stars, thinking of what might have been. In a few minutes we would crawl into the unmarked van waiting for us in the marina parking lot and assume new identities, new hobbies, and new friends. Everything about my old life would disappear.

Maybe it was better this way. My hunt for real supernatural stories had nearly killed my sister. And it *had* killed me. At least that's the way the news media was playing it up. "Young teen drowns in creek, details at eleven." *Which is right about now,* I thought. I had no way of knowing if Gabrovski would believe the news reports. Probably not. Except for calling to Dad from that thicket, I had given Gabrovski no reason to suspect I was anything other than dead.

But he was crafty and smart — the worst kind of monster.

Calvin had agreed to run a disclaimer on the website explaining that, in honor of me and my contribution to the site, he and others on the editorial staff had collaborated on my final article for the *Cool Ghoul Gazette*. I felt a twinge of regret knowing others were taking credit for my writing, but oh well. Death happens.

"The thing about living and dying is this," Dirk had explained earlier that day. We had left the beach and were walking back to the parking lot. "Let's say you are God and you created everything. The sky and earth and people. Now suppose the creatures you created have some really whacked-out ideas of who God is. In fact, a lot of them don't even think you are real. So one day you decide to come down and explain to them what life and death and life after death is all about. Because you're God and they're just creatures you created, they would never be able to comprehend how awesome you are. So to make things easy for these poor creatures you created, you write yourself into their story. You call it His Story. And when you show up on earth you tell everyone you are God's Son. You tell everyone you meet that you are the exact replica of God: that if they like the Son they'll love the Father. But they don't believe you. And why would they? People have their own ideas about who God is and this person calling himself God's Son doesn't fit their idea of what God is like. So they kill you. But then you do something that blows them away. You go back to heaven and send your Spirit to earth. Except, only those that really want to find Jesus and receive his Holy Spirit."

"What does this have to do with living and dying?" I'd asked.

"Don't you see? We're all zombies. Or I should say you are until you get God's Spirit in you. You might walk around like you are alive, but really you're dead. Dead because of the curse. And you'll remain in the realm of the dead forever unless you get God's Spirit. Anyway, that's my take on living and dying and life after death."

"Hey, look at you sitting up there like Captain Sparrow." I whirled in the chair. A figure stood on the dock, the silhouette banked against the dock lights. "Permission to come aboard?"

"Granted." I rose and reached out, taking Kat's hand in mine as I pulled her aboard. "Took you long enough."

"They had to check my lungs. Wanted to make sure I hadn't ingested dirt. If I had and it settled in my lungs, that could lead to pneumonia, which in turn might lead to ..."

"Yeah, yeah, I know. But we were just about to take off. I was sitting thinking I might not get to say good-bye."

"Aw, that's sweet. You waiting around for me."

Without responding I walked Kat to the back of the boat. She sat, her eyes looking up into mine. "Well?"

"Give me a second. I want to enjoy this."

"What?"

"Looking at you."

In the glow of lights I saw her cheeks redden. She tugged on my hand, pulling me onto the bench. I sat close beside her, our bare feet touching.

More cars were arriving in the parking lot. Boat owners, I guessed, arriving for the weekend.

"So what's on your mind?"

"You mostly. I wanted to say I'm sorry. I never should have asked you to ..." I squeezed her hand, choking down the rest of my words.

"It's not your fault, Kansas; you cudden have done nothing even if you'd tried."

Taking a deep breath, I uncoiled my fingers and rubbed the back of her knuckles with my thumb. "Officer McDonald got shot and almost died—how's that not my fault? Poke Salad Annie ended up in the hospital with a concussion from where she whacked her head on the ground—that's on me. Then there's you."

"Dudden matter, Kansas, dudden matter a'tall. I ain't dead. Yet. That's all a body can hope for. Now stop beating yourself up." Kat thumped me on the shoulder. "That's my job."

We laughed together and in doing so I suddenly felt exhausted.

Kat said, "You took a big risk telling Officer McDonald about who you suspected. How did you know *he* waden the one holding your sister?"

"I wasn't 100 percent certain, but I had to trust somebody. Officer McDonald seemed honestly shocked to learn a killer was renting his townhome. On our ride back to the marina, we both agreed that our best chance for finding Wendy was for me to be the bait. I was afraid my parents might make me go with them to the motel, but Officer McDonald came to bat for me. He explained that me hanging around the marina might be a good idea. You know, in case Wendy returned, which we both knew by then was not going to happen. He made sure Matthew

Carter knew I was going to Poke Salad Annie's place. Our hope was Carter would tell Gabrovski. Our plan nearly worked."

"But not quite," Kat declared.

"No, not quite. When Carter showed up dressed like Heidi May Laveau, I thought I'd misjudged things. But then all of a sudden Gabrovski pushed Carter into that pit. I thought the boy was dead for sure. Especially given the way he landed. Sounded like he'd broken his neck. Then later when I came back to the fire pit and found you gone and him shoveling dirt into that pit ..."

The words caught in my throat. I swallowed and looked away.

"'Round these parts we got lots of possums. They're like the Palmetto Island mascot. Thing you learn from a possum is how to play dead. I've seen 'em dragged out of a chicken coop by the tail and flung into a ditch. Next thing you know they done jumped up and run off. When you're dead you stay dead, so I played dead."

"But the first time I saw you tied to that tree, you didn't move, not even a little."

"He thought he'd killed me, he really did. When I came back for you after work and stepped out of that boat, he clubbed me with that shovel. I saw stars, he hit me so hard. Didn't knock me out, but it hurt like the devil. So I give him what he wanted: a dead Kat."

"Hey, that's a good one, dead cat."

Kat rested her head on my shoulder and breathed a sigh

that could have passed for purring. She remained quiet for a long time, then lifted her head and kissed my cheek. "Thanks for saving me."

"No problem."

"I mean it, Kansas." Her breath felt warm against my ear. "Other than my dad, you're the only real hero I've ever known." She rested her cheek against mine and breathed a sigh that reached to the heavens.

I hoped her tears were not contagious. I didn't want to be known as the mushy Nick Caden from Kansas. Or for Kat to know how much I cared.

"Close your eyes."

"You're not going to kiss me, are you?"

"Wouldn't be the worst thing to ever happen to you. Now close your eyes, Kansas."

I closed my eyes. She pulled away. I heard a crackling sound like plastic wrapping. Two curved, hard lips pressed against mine. I nibbled the chocolaty sweetness.

"Mmm, I like." My tongue probed the mushy softness. With my eyes still closed, I asked, "Moon Pie?"

"God's food," Kat answered. "Don't get no better than that." She pushed the round chocolate-coated graham cracker sandwich into my mouth. "Something to remember me by."

"Oooh, yuck!"

Startled, I opened my eyes. Kat held the other half of the Moon Pie in her mouth, our noses inches apart. My sister stood on the dock, pointing at us.

"Dad, Nick is kissing a girl!"

"Was not!"

"Was too!"

"They're ready for us, son." Dad looked proud. And a little sad. But mostly he looked tired. "It's time to go."

Kat pulled back, ran her fingers through her hair, and gave me a quick peck on the cheek. "See you 'round, Kansas. You're 'bout the best thing that's ever happened to Palmetto. And me."

Suddenly she was gone.

I gathered myself, tamped down the sadness, and joined my family on the dock. The Nick I'd known was gone, too. Dead, thanks to Gabrovski. Dead and buried and filed away with an obit.

But who knows. Maybe Nick Caden will rise again. Could happen.

In a world where the dead don't stay dead, anything is possible.

## Dead Man's Hand

*Eddie Jones*

Nick Caden's vacation at Deadwood Canyon Ghost Town takes a deadly turn toward trouble when the fourteen-year-old finds himself trapped in a livery stable with the infamous outlaw Jesse James. The shooter whirls, aims and… vanishes. *Great theatrics*, Nick thinks, except now he's alone in the hayloft with the bullet-riddled body of Billy the Kid. And by the time the sheriff arrives, the body disappears.

Soon Nick is caught in a deadly chase—from an abandoned gold mine, through forbidden buffalo hunting grounds, and across Rattlesnake Gulch. Around every turn he finds another suspect. Will Nick solve the murder? Will his parents have him committed? Or will the town's infatuation with Hollywood theatrics conceal the real truth about souls, spirits and the destiny that awaits those who die.

## Skull Creek Stakeout

*Eddie Jones*

After solving the Deadwood mystery, Nick lands a job as a roving reporter for The Cool Ghoul Gazette, a website on paranormal disturbances. When the editor sends Nick to investigate a murder, Nick finds a corpse sporting fangs, bite marks, and a gaping hole in its chest, courtesy of a wooden stake.

Will Nick unravel the truth behind the "blood covenant," or will his new job suck the life out of him?

Nick Caden has a "supernatural" knack for finding trouble. He's a normal fourteen-year-old who attracts ghosts, vampires, and the undead—or so it seems. But Nick's relentless search for truth leads him into worlds of darkness with grave consequences, where the dead, dying, and deranged walk… on really hot coals.

*Available in stores and online!*

## ZONDERVAN®
.com